BEYOND
RESILIENCE

RECREATE YOUR LIFE WITH LOVE

GANESH BABU

Contents

Author's Note

This is a work of fiction. All the names, characters, places, and incidents are either the products of the author's imagination or used facetiously and are not to be constructed as real. Any resemblance to actual events, locals, organizations, or people, living or dead, is entirely coincidental.

Preface

It was about 11 o'clock at night when I was on my way from Vila Madalena to Santo Amaro in the city of Sao Paulo, Brazil. It was just like the other day; I casually took the staircase in the metro to get to the other side of the road. There I saw a gringo, looking terrified, and a man was standing behind her. At that moment, I didn't have anything in my mind; I just thought that she was lost and trying to figure out a way. So, I casually walked toward her and asked if she needed any help. Being a foreigner, I was able to understand how it feels to be lost in a place where we can't speak the local language, and having a fear of getting mobbed would be even worse. As I approached her in English, she immediately recognized that I was a foreigner too. She engaged in a conversation with me and asked if I could go with her to the nearest shopping center. I lived just half a kilometer away from that place, and I could also sense the fear and tension in her voice, so I told her, "Okay." As we got out of the station, she started crying, and I had no clue what was happening. I tried to calm her down and assured her that she was safe. After a long pause, she started sharing what had happened to her in the metro; she was followed by a man who was standing behind her, tried pulling her jacket, and used some abusive words too. She was terrified and badly in need of help. In the same conversation, she also shared similar stories which happened to her and some of her friends back in Houston, Texas. She told me that none of the counties is safe for women, neither Sweden nor Denmark, "Women are always an easy target for men." I told her that in the first week of my stay in Sao Paulo, I was also afraid to go to certain places and travel alone, especially at night. It was petrifying. Eventually, I got used to it, and now, I'm on my own. She asked me, "What were you afraid of?" I said I was afraid of losing my cell phone and some cash I had on me. She laughed at me and said, "Well, that clearly distinguished the fear of men and women. More than losing belongings, women are afraid of being touched, molested, and raped." I could neither deny nor did I disagree with her, and what she said made sense to me. Just a few minutes of conversation with her had a tremendous impact on me, and my concern about domestic violence and sexual harassment had augmented. So, I started paying attention to it, talked to both men and women to know their views, and read more articles as well.

Two weeks later, I accidentally met the same girl at the bus stop; she was standing on the other side of the road and somehow recognized me and called me out loud but couldn't grab my attention. She immediately crossed the road to get hold of me before I boarded the bus. We had a cup of coffee at the nearby cafe. She was constantly exposing her aversion toward all men, including her stepfather. "Gender-based hypocrisy is on the rise in our society; it's perfectly portrayed that women are equally given opportunities, for example, female president, women in the space and voting rights, etc., but in reality, these are just brainwashing," she added. She is a Christian feminist who believed that Jesus was the first person who raised his voice for women and fought against gender-based violence. She also stated that the world is infested by men, and women are just prey for them by all means. "If you don't like any men, then why are you spending time with me in the cafe?" "I'm not a disloyal person. You helped me when I was in need of it, so I wanted to thank you. That's why I invited you for coffee."

Sometimes, as human beings, we don't understand the fact that we are becoming the byproduct of what we see, hear, and experience in our lives. We all are a stack of accumulation, be it food or emotion; our actions and opinions are based on the accretion of our past life because we consciously or unconsciously built a one-way container in our minds with a firmly sealed base, so whatever that life throws at us, either good or bad, gets stuck in it. It plays a significant role in controlling the rest of our journey in this world. We can't keep our container empty, which is practically impossible because, as human beings, we have the power of evocation as it's our inborn nature. It's just that we need to have a baseless container that will not let anything stay permanently, so there will be no impact on future events. However, acquiring wisdom from the bitter experience in our past becomes essential to avoid the same mistake all over again. Her stepfather sexually abused her, and the similar stories of her friends and other bitter experiences of harassment and abuse in her life have turned her against all the men in the world.

I didn't get involved in any sort of argument proving that there are good men too. Rather, I just listened to her because I could understand what she had gone through and how it completely changed her thoughts. I talked about this to one of my friends and told her the fact that I'm speaking with people, including victims and non-victims, and also doing a lot of research to know more about sexual harassment. She asked me what I was going to do about it, and I replied, "No idea." She laughed at me and said, "Can I suggest you something if you don't mind?" I said, "Of course." She told me to write a book.

I had never thought of writing a book or being an author, but what she said made sense to me. I considered that and started working on my thought process and did my research for two years to know the mindset of both men and women so that I could give an authentic product to the world. After setting down successfully and halfway through the book, I had to write some important scenes of the story, which needed the opinions of both victims and the common people. It was really fascinating to know that most of the victims had no intention of taking revenge, but they still held grudges and brooded over them. On the other hand, when I narrated the story to the non-victims to know their opinion on how they wanted it to proceed, they reacted a lot with the feeling of retaliation. With great respect for their views and opinions, I completed the story with the help of many wonderful people. This book could be a duster to remove the painful past and an eye-opener for people who want to start a new life of their dreams.

Chapter 1

Embracing Motherhood

The sky turns gray as the clouds gather, and the day becomes dark as it gets older. The kisses of drizzles on the land of Rockville bring out a beautiful, earthy smell. A gentle blow of wind has swooped the northern cardinals and American robins. Witnessing them murmur is a gift for one's eyes. But the mood of the situation gradually changes when precipitation picks up and the unwelcome guest from the sky has gotten people indoors in town. Yet the heavily expectant mother on the porch forgets all her pain, anguish, and torments of her past in the acrobatic behavior of Mother Nature. She gently holds her nine-month-old baby bump in one hand, closes her eyes with her chin up in ecstasy, and extends the other hand to catch water sliding from the rooftop of her house. She is playing with the water like a five-year-old child, but she can't decipher the message it carries. Suddenly, a lightning strike brings her back to the real world. The wind becomes stronger, and the downpour becomes heavier; the wet and slippery corridor has made it hard for her swollen feet to get into the house. Her heart beats louder than the shattering windows; the continuous thunder and lightning frighten her to the core. Sandra Jones; is a young parturient woman who has experienced things that most women wouldn't have dreamed of in their lives, but her determination has helped to paddle across the strong waves, yet her battle continues. Being alone by choice is a gift of solitude that one can accord to oneself; it's the greatest feeling that only a few people can relish, whereas undesired loneliness and imposition of isolation from the world is a curse of a cross that most people endure. Sandra's life may seem like a malison, but her attitude toward adversity is different because she is a very positive woman.

It's about 9 p.m., and it is still raining. Sandra senses the signs of an accouchement. "Oh my god, it's going to happen." She's panicking and tries to find her cell phone to get some help. Unfortunately, a sudden roar of thunder gets her water broken and increases her fear of dropping the baby on the floor. She lies down on the carpet as the pain is unbearable, and screams loudly due to contractions. The distance between the houses is quite far as it is situated on the outskirts of the town, so her screams go unheard. She is a strong and brave woman who can even dare to take on a grown lion. But the lashes of labor pangs are intolerable for every woman, and Sandra is no exception. As the pain rises, she tries to fight back her tears but still can't bear the acute stings, so she decides to divert her mind. To be able to divert one's mind during labor is practically impossible; however, Sandra manages to wade through it because she is so strong in her spirit.

After hours of struggle, she takes a deep breath and pushes the baby down with her willpower. The bundle of joy has come sliding out of her. Finally, she could hear the cry of her baby. Reviving from the fatigue of her body, she manages to see the face of the cute baby girl and calls her, "Merlin, my little princess."

On the one hand, Sandra is amazed by the gorgeous seven-pound beauty that God has sent into her life. But on the other hand, she is worried that she's a girl child and has to live in this merciless society. The soft, tender hands, pale skin, fragile body, and smile of her baby have strengthened her to sit by herself and take the infant in her hands. Her joy is so immense that she's forgotten her pain.

Sandra believes that the entire planet is highly patriarchal, so she was afraid of the throttles that Merlin might have to face in her life. In her eyes, the world is so cruel to women, and bringing her child to this terrible place gives her nightmares.

Days pass by, and the nature around her, such as the magnificent landscape surrounded by water bodies, bumpy hills, skyscraping trees, and humongous greenery, helped Sandra to recover faster. The amazing scenery became the glue to her broken heart and healed her quickly.

After a few months of maternity leave, Sandra is back on her feet and travels back to Baltimore, Maryland, to join her work. Being a single mom, it has become even more challenging as she's supposed to play the roles of both mother and father. She leaves her daughter in the daycare center and goes to work. To her surprise, she has been replaced by other women at her designation without any prior notice. She had already expected something like this would happen, but still, it was a bolt from the blue. Sandra is unable to leave her job as it's the only bread and butter for her family. The sudden demotion in designation has made her very upset and spends some time in the cafeteria with a cup of coffee and starts to think about how to handle it. She's unexpectedly interrupted by a phone call from the daycare center.

"Hi, Ms. Sandra; I wanna tell you something. It's very urgent," says the nanny.

"Yes, please," says Sandra.

"Ma'am, your daughter had a seizure and is at the Nurses Station. Please come immediately," says the nanny.

"Oh my god! What happened? Is she okay? I'm coming there right now," says Sandra.

Sandra doesn't have time to think about anything else but wonders how to get permission from her boss Michael. She has to go to see her daughter immediately. As there is no other option left, she makes up her mind, goes to him, and explains her situation, but he doesn't seem to understand it. Michael gives her two choices.

"You can either go to your daughter and never come back or just carry on with your work and leave after office hours."

Sandra is aware of his intention and knows that he won't let her work in peace. So, without uttering a word, she goes straight to her cabin, picks up all her personal stuff, and drops her office keys at his desk with a fierce look to let him know that she has burned her bridge. She boards a bus that heads toward the daycare center and sits next to a window seat. Being jobless and broke with the news that she received from the nanny has knocked her over; Sandra is very upset about the unconscionable action that Michael has taken against her, in spite of knowing her brilliance and loyalty. She closes her eyes and starts thinking about what happened during her maternity leave.

* * *

After she was discharged from the hospital with her baby, Michael came to pay her a visit to Rockville. Despite the fact that she had just recovered from cramps, he tried to take advantage of her. While she was nursing the baby, he got closer to kiss the child, but she immediately pushed him away.

"Are you crazy? Do you want to die as an assistant? If you cooperate with me just for tonight, you will get your promotion," said Michael.

"What do you want to do with me now? Do you have any idea what I had gone through to get this baby out of my womb? Listen! I don't want to trade my body to get any promotion. You can't bribe all women to fulfill your needs. I'm warning you now. Just get away from my sight; otherwise, I will not hesitate to use the knife to cut your throat," said Sandra.

Michael didn't try to ravish her because he knew what she was capable of. With great frustration at not being able to do what he'd intended, he uttered, "You will face the consequences." He walked away livid.

* * *

Now Sandra opens her eyes, and the bus arrives at the crèche. As soon as the bus stops, she runs with anxiety to the Nurses Station and spots the nanny who is waiting for her at the reception.

"How is my child? Where is she?" asks Sandra nervously.

"Please, don't panic, ma'am. It was an emergency; there was no time to even think of what to do, so we rushed her to the hospital," replies the nanny.

Sandra becomes distressed after hearing the news that her daughter is in the emergency room; her heart pounds a mile a minute, and tears roll down her cheeks. She goes to the hospital, which is just a few blocks away, and sits beside her daughter's bed, slowly running her hand into her child's curly hair. As she gets closer, her tears drop on the soft cheek of her baby, which awakens Merlin from sleep. Merlin opens her eyes and feels excited to see her mother sitting next to her. She hugs and kisses her all over the face.

Sandra loves her daughter so much as she's everything to her. Every day she prays to God to make this world a better place, not only for Merlin but for all women.

Days turned into weeks, and weeks turned into months. She has exhausted almost all the money that she has squirreled away.

The doorbell rings, and it's 6 a.m.

Sandra jumps out of bed to see who's out there so early in the morning. She gently opens the door, only to be pushed back into the room by her landlady's husband. The door is left wide open, and Sandra walks backward while the man forces himself on her before she can react. Suddenly, the landlady walks in, only to discover them standing too close to each other. He promptly withdraws himself since he saw his wife through a window mirror and says, "I've just come here to ask for rent as it's been due for months. She's trying to entice me with sex-for-rent because she cannot afford to pay us anymore." Without even analyzing the situation or verifying the truth from both of them, the owner yells out, saying, "This is why I don't rent my houses to single women." When Sandra tries to justify herself, she is overruled by the landlady. "I had been patient with you even though the rent is due for the past six months, but to keep a woman of no character would ruin my married life. I want to evict you right away, but I'm not ruthless, hence a week's time notice, nothing more for you, to find another house and vacate my place."

"Like eating a lot of junk food, most of us consume the indignity that people throw at us. Both are not good for your health. One would get you fatter, and the other would get you depressed; they could even kill you eventually. Some people are meant to throw trash at you. Just avoid them and delete them from your contact list. When you're on a diet, you're conscious of what you eat. Similarly, you should be aware of the people you let into your life. Because the people you associate with have the power to make or break your life. Unhealthy food and hostile people are both a piece of garbage and a waste of time"

Sandra's been kicked out of the house not because she was accused of seducing a man to rule out the rent but to save the lives of two women from a man of no morals. Sometimes, the mist of insecurity will blur out the unprejudiced wisdom. The landlord clearly knows what would've happened in the first place, but the precariousness of life has pushed her to do injustice.

The words of the landlord are swarming in her head; Church is the only place where Sandra can find peace and happiness, so she goes to a nearby Chapel. Holding Merlin in her arms and kneeling to pray, she is unable to express her thoughts in words, but more than that, her tears express her grief. With nowhere to go, no one to trust, and no shoulder to lean upon, she puts her trust in God.

Prayer is her only strength; it empowers her to endure the unjust things that have happened as well as motivates her to live each day. Almost after an hour of prayer, she gets up, walks through the wooden door where she sees a notice board, and learns that there is a job vacancy at York Shrine church. Sandra feels her prayers are answered; she quickly makes a note of the address and phone number. Life has taught her to stoop down to any extent as long as there is integrity, even if she has to live off the roads. Yet she can't imagine the sight of her baby being raised on the pavement. She could've removed the entire poster from the notice board so that other people couldn't apply for that job, but she doesn't do that. Because she believes that if it's yours, it's yours, and nobody can grab it from you. If you don't get it, then it's not meant for you. Sandra is constantly reminding herself that they are practically homeless and are desperately in search of food as well as shelter. Without any delay, she starts to walk as she can't afford to hail a cab. On foot, it takes her two hours to get to Jackson Town, where the church is located. Carrying the baby in her arm is quite a challenge. Persistence and mindfulness are her key characteristics, so the journey continues.

Upon reaching her destination and without any further ado, she sits with her daughter and waits for the opportunity to talk to the Father in person. Sandra is the kind of woman who'd never scrounge up regardless of her situation. It's her inborn nature, a woman of true moral value. She believes in getting things out of integrity and merit.

"Father, may I have a word with you?" says Sandra.

"Of course, my child! What is it about?" says the Father.

She tells Father that she's seen a job vacancy posted on the church notice board and would like to apply for it. "I've two years of experience volunteering in Faith Baptist church at Swinburne when I was a teenager, and I also studied in a bible school. I'm wondering if I could get a job here," asks Sandra.

"The church actually needs a person who can manage the directory of all the homeless people. If you are interested in taking this job, you will be paid $750 for the first six months. After your probation period, based on your dedication and attitude, you will get a raise of $250 in addition," says the pastor.

Even though it's a meager pay, she doesn't consider it a pittance. It means a lot to her, and she accepts it with gratitude.

"Thank you so much, Father. You've not only given me a job but also the confidence to live my life, and I'm really grateful to take this wonderful opportunity. Thank you once again for considering me a right match for this position," says Sandra.

"If you want to thank somebody, thank our Almighty," says Father Williams.

Luckily, Sandra gets the offer and is asked to take the position the very next day. With a thankful heart, she walks enthusiastically, not feeling the tiredness she has walked miles back and forth, and still gleaming with joy.

Being strapped for cash and only able to buy food for her child, she just drinks a glass of water to elude starvation. As happy and thrilled to start the first day of work in the most gracious place, Sandra feels like she has everything from soup to nuts, but in reality, she just has plain water. With loads of excitement, she hits the bed on time, as tomorrow will be a big day for her. The next morning, she's all set and heads to Chapel on foot. At the church office, she marvels at her work on the first day itself. She walks up and down the staircase, gets her station cleaned, has attended more than fifty phone calls, and booked ten appointments for the presbyter.

Although she's up in her spirit of having found a job in a holy place, the deadline that her landlord had given to move out of the house is haunting her constantly. Ravenous and enervated, and has not eaten many meals, ambulated to-and-fro for quite a distance, and, being assiduous at work, has exerted herself a lot. She suddenly collapses while trudging the last few steps on the staircase to get to the registry room. With the phone ringing off the hook, Father William and the presbyter walk in to check why no one answers the phone and wonder what Sandra is doing. They are alarmed to see her in an unconscious state, lying on the floor, and trying to revive her immediately, but she doesn't have the strength even to open her eyes.

One of them quickly dials 911 and asks for an ambulance. Paramedics arrive and diagnose that she's dehydrated and must not have eaten for days. She is put on an IV drip, and her condition stabilizes. She clearly knows that a slice of bread and a glass of milk will bring her back on foot, so a recommended hospital stay is refused. Father William is now interrogating her about why she hasn't eaten and where she lives. Sandra is initially a bit reluctant, but upon insistence, she tells Father that she is jobless, broke, and the deadline that her landlord has given to move out, and walking for miles with no food has conked her out. She's immediately given a glass of milk and some toast.

"Why didn't you tell me all this beforehand? Did you think that I'd turn my back?" says Father.

"No, no, certainly not, Father. When I came out of the church with a heavy heart, I was in dire need of a job and saw the advertisement for a vacancy. I didn't even know whether or not I would get it. You believed me and gave me a job instantly without asking any questions. My prayers are answered, and I'm sure God will get us a place to stay and food to eat."

"You are so right; God has just given you a roof over your head and a meal on your plate. You may stay here with us. The church will provide you with food and shelter as long as your service continues. I've been watching you since morning. Although you have had many problems in your life, you are still sincere and unpretentious, which is absolutely remarkable. You hadn't just availed this free bed and board as you're in a dire situation, but it's a reward for your dedication and integrity."

Sandra loves her current job. Now, she doesn't have to put Merlin in the daycare as there are many people to look after the child. York Shrine is one of the oldest and most historic churches in town; it accommodates thousands of people every month and serves free food for the homeless. Everyone in the church loves Merlin, and she enjoys being there too. Sandra becomes busy with her daily tasks, but her hatred for men and resentment against them never go away.

Chapter 2

The Chase

The phone rings. "York Shrine church, how may I help you?" asks Sandra.

"Hello, my child! Father Williams here. I'd like to have a word with you. Please come to my office."

"Of course, Father," says Sandra.

She immediately goes to Father William's office room.

"Please have a seat, my child," says the pastor and continues, "It's been almost six months since you started working here as a registrar in our church. I like your work, and we are so fortunate to have a blessed person like you. To be honest with you, Sandra, before you got appointed here, nothing was organized, and there was no track of who was coming in and going out. It concerned me a lot, but now everything is in the right order in God's house. May you be blessed, my child!"

Sandra becomes emotional and says, "Father, I still can't forget those days I used to walk for hours without food to get here. Both my child and I were in a state of complete destitution, and there was no one to harbor us. If you hadn't given me an opportunity to work as a registrar in this most beautiful place, I wonder where I'd have ended up with my daughter. I'm really indebted to you and the church for providing us with food and shelter."

"You're in safe hands, my child. Don't worry about anything," says Father Williams.

Sandra has to get back to her desk to complete some pending work. A man walks in as soon as she leaves Father's office room. He enters the room without Father's permission and shows him a picture.

"Have you seen this woman?" asks the man.

"Who are you, and what do you want?" Father Williams asks in a fearful voice.

"I need this woman; I heard she lives in this town. Does she visit this church?" says the man with a loud and firm voice.

"I don't know what you are talking about, gentleman. I've never seen her before," says Father with a shaky voice.

He holds Father Williams by the collar, pushes him against the wall, and points a gun at him. With fear and pain, Father tells him, "The lady you are looking for is not here. If I happen to see her, I'll let you know." "You better inform me if you know anything about her. Otherwise, I will never spare anyone in this church." The man reluctantly lets go of his collar and walks out on him impertinently as he does not get an appealing answer.

A great sigh of relief! Father Williams couldn't believe what had just happened, and it took him a while to recover from the shock. He looks at the main gate of the church to make sure that the man leaves. He immediately calls the security guard and says, "Don't allow anybody inside without my permission, and keep the gates closed."

He can't wait to enquire Sandra about the man who has just scared him to death. So, he phones her right away, but the call reaches voicemail: "Sandra, I need to talk to you. Please come to my room; it's an emergency." Father Williams becomes restless and calls Sandra multiple times, but it ends up reaching her voicemail. He also texts her: "CALL ME WHEN YOU SEE THIS MESSAGE. IT'S URGENT!"

Sandra calls the pastor's cell phone as soon as she reads the message.

"Hello, Father. I am sorry I missed your call. Please tell me," says Sandra.

"That's fine. Please come to my office immediately," asks Father Williams.

"Okay, Father," says Sandra.

"All right, I want to ask you something very important. After you spoke with me, a man came to my office with your photo and inquired about you. I pretended that I had never seen you before because he didn't look like a man of honor. I didn't want to put your life at stake."

"Did he tell you his name, Father?" says Sandra.

Although it's been just six months since she joined, her integrity has been greatly admired by Father Williams. She has changed the total structure of the church and made it well organized. If he'd blindly trust anybody, it'd only be Sandra. So, he politely answers her question rather than interrogating her.

"No, he didn't, and I didn't dare to ask him, but he gave me a small piece of paper with his phone number to inform him about your whereabouts. I can vividly remember his physical appearance, and I'm sure I can perfectly describe him. He is about six-foot tall, thin, with long hair like a hippie, and has a heavy accent. He should be in his late sixties."

Sandra starts muddling and says to herself, "How come he found me? He's come so far searching for me. Does he know about Merlin? Oh my god!" Her mind races over thoughts and gets nervous.

She looks stressed and breaks out in a sweat as if she struggled up the hill. The Father surmises that there is something terribly wrong and continues, "I have got a very important meeting to address. People are waiting for me in the conference room; I can't cancel it now. Don't worry about anything. We're by your side. Don't run any personal errands for at least the next few days. I'm afraid he'd be around looking for you. I will talk to you right after I finish my meeting. Please be available; I need to talk to you in detail." Sandra does not utter a word but goes straight to see her daughter to make sure that she's all right. But to her surprise, Merlin is not there in her crib. She thoroughly checks the entire building and asks everyone in the church if they have seen her daughter around, but no one has. Without wasting a moment, she dials Father's cell phone. "Merlin is missing; I can't find her anywhere. Did you see him leaving the premises? Was he alone, or did he have Merlin in his hand?" asks Sandra.

"No, I saw him leaving our premises all by himself," says the pastor.

In York Shrine church, there's a woman called Maria who became a close friend to Sandra during their stay. Merlin spends most of her time with Maria, especially when her mother is busy registering new entries. She usually takes the child to the park, which is less than half a kilometer away from the church. It's one of the biggest parks in town, but only a few people visit there because it's a place for conducting illegal activities. People also call it a crack house, and there has been a police riot recently. Four men were shot dead during a clash between two gangs. The government just reopened the park after it had been temporarily closed. Although Maria is advised not to take the child to the park, she continues spending time there with the kid in mere negligence. Sandra thinks she must be at the park with her daughter, so she runs fast to see if she has gotten Merlin there. As she enters, the big old trees at the park border the fields and act like guards, muffling the sound of the busy street around them. This makes the place calm and peaceful and also suitable for doing unlawful acts, unfortunately. Maria spends most of her time here as it's very quiet and isolated from the rest of the world. Sandra is calling out their names and searching for them everywhere; there's an old couple walking by on the pathway opposite Sandra. She promptly sprints to them to ask if they have seen both Maria and Merlin. One of them says, "There was a woman in her thirties, wearing a brown top and a dark green skirt with a child in her arms. It looked like she was scuttling from someone. After some time, a man lunged at us and inquired about the same woman and the child, but he sounded more horrendous, so we didn't respond to his questions." Sandra asks if they have seen them going out of the park, but they haven't.

"Is there a way out on the other side of the park? Because they might have exited that way," asks Sandra.

"Yes, there is, but that's an abandoned gate. Nobody uses it," says the duo.

Sandra is suffocating in fear as if someone is choking her to death. Without uttering another word, she rushes into the park to save her daughter and her friend. As she goes farther into the park, it turns out to be a forest inhabiting broad-leaved and thorn woodland, copses, thickets, and bushland. It gets darker as the trees on either side are covered up, and the sunlight hardly reaches the ground through the dapples of leaves. She gasps hard to catch her breath, yet she continues to walk without a halt and shouts their names loudly. The path gets narrow, and there's no sign of anybody. The only sound she can hear is the rustling leaves and birds fluttering among them. At the far end, there is a dilapidated abode. Sandra is neither worried about her own life nor does she think of going back to the church. All she has on her mind right now is to save her daughter and friend and take them back to the church safely. There she sees a forsaken house and walks toward it to check if they're hiding inside; nobody can ever imagine spending even a minute in that terrible place. The derelict appearance would frighten anybody who wants to get in.

She stands in front of the rotten wooden door with a rusted metal handle. With great trepidation, she twists the knob of the door. It creaks. The sound that echoes fills the room; it would cause any heart to skip a beat. She silently pads into the living room and carefully investigates if someone is there. But this time, they are not being preconized by her as it would alert the man who might be at the same house looking for them. There's a flight of old, warped stairs ahead of her which leads to another room. It's quite risky to take those steps as they might give way, but it doesn't sway her determination to make it to the second floor. She can hear the creak from underneath as she gets on the staircase. The creaking sound gets louder to the further steps, and her hands are wrapped up in the old wooden banister. Alas, somehow, she manages to reach there, but the door is locked from the inside. Her intuition says they must be hiding there. Now, she gets a ray of hope and remembers the wonderful lines that her mother used to say. "Your prayers are your strength; you may not know how powerful it is, but they'll certainly give you the wisdom of light, which will brighten your path when you are surrounded by darkness." Keeping those lines in mind, she breaks open the door. When she observes a closet in the corner of the room that appears to be slightly moving, as if someone is hiding inside, her heart begins to race. But Sandra can sense it must be Maria and Merlin hiding inside, so she gently taps it. "Maria, Merlin... you guys are safe; this is Sandra, I have come to save you guys, and I know you are hiding inside. Please come out, please come out," quavers Sandra with tears rolling down. There they are, sitting inside the closet, shivering and shaking.

Sandra forgets all her anguish and fears the moment she sees her daughter's face. They couldn't wait any longer to hug each other; Maria couldn't stop crying and barely said a word.

"What happened to Merlin? Why doesn't she open her eyes?" She pats her cheeks gently to help her gain consciousness. Merlin slowly opens her eyes, and in the excitement of seeing her mother, she starts crying loudly; Maria closes her mouth and says, "Honey, please, don't make a noise; we need to leave this place as fast as we can. Otherwise, none of us will survive. I know the shortest way, so please follow me." Although Maria knew all the nooks and corners of the park, she couldn't get away as he closely chased her. Somehow, she manages to lose him and ends up in the abandoned house. To their luck, he was misled into the maze of confusion and headed to the other side of the park. The sound of Sandra's footsteps made Maria speculate that it could be him, which forced her to be locked up in the room and hide inside the closet with the child. Both Sandra and Maria have a lot of questions to ask each other, but all they want now is to get to the church safely. The serenity in the aftermath of the horrible hunt is remarkable for all three of them.

Pastor Williams is impatiently waiting at the gate and looking at the far end of the road to see if there is any sign of their arrival. There they come; Sandra carries her daughter and holds Maria by her hand. He's so happy to see them coming and goes to the prayer hall to thank God for bringing them back safely. Their panics have been temporarily arrested.

"What happened? Where was Merlin? How did you meet Maria? Is Merlin all right?" asks Father nervously. Sandra and Maria look exhausted while Merlin's fast asleep. Sandra tells him that she found Maria and Merlin in Benedict Park. Father gets mad at Maria as soon as he hears the name of the park. "That's literally a crack house. I told you many times not to go there, but despite my warnings, you took the child to the park. We are here to protect the people who are in our shelter and not to put their lives in danger." Sandra jumps in immediately and tells Father Williams, "I'm sorry, Father. There's a misunderstanding. She's actually saved Merlin's life." "I'm sorry, Maria. I didn't mean to..." apologizes Sandra. "That's okay. It was my fault. I shouldn't have created that impression." "Since it's a pressing problem, a question of life and death that disturbs our harmonious lives here, I need an elaborate explanation from each one of you. After which, I need to talk to the presbyter and take the necessary precautions, and we also have to get help from the cops. I already instructed the security guard not to allow anybody into the premises." Suddenly, Maria faints on the floor. Both Father Williams and Sandra are shocked. They fetch a glass of water and sprinkle it over her face. Sandra feeds her some water, and she revives instantly. "Are you all right? Shall I call the doctor?" "No need of that, Father. It's just that I'm starving and worn out from the incident." "Oh my god! You have not had anything. It was my bad. I was worried about you all, so I totally forgot everything."

"Have your dinner and go to sleep. It's quite late to discuss anything. We shall talk tomorrow morning. Thank god for the blessings that you have had." Father Williams looks into Sandra's eyes and says, "We need to talk tomorrow."

Father Williams calls them to his room the following day, and they all sit together. First, Father asks, "Maria, what happened? How did you guys end up in the park? How did he get to you?"

"Merlin and I were feeding the pigeons. Suddenly, a guy appeared out of the blue. I'd never seen him before in our neighborhood. He was very tall and was wearing a long black coat and a hat; he looked very suspicious," says Maria and continues, "He got closer to us, pulled a picture of Sandra from his jacket, and asked me with a brutal voice if I'd seen her around here. I hastily said, 'No.' Unfortunately, Merlin saw the picture and cried, 'Mumma.' That rang the bell in his mind. He immediately got hold of us, took out a gun from his jacket, and said, 'I've been hunting for this woman for a long time. Give me the child, now.' He tried to drag Merlin from me. I pushed him away and ran into the park. As I had been there many times and explored all the places, I could get rid of him. I was totally devastated and despaired before I saw Sandra in that room. Luckily, he doesn't know I work here; otherwise, having Merlin in my hand would have definitely brought him back to the church. Sandra came at the right time to save our skin. When she entered the room, I thought it was him. I can't forget that horrible moment; it was such a nightmare."

Father Williams looks into Sandra's eyes. She has to tell him who the man is and why he's looking for her. "Sandra, you need to tell us everything so that we can help you out. I'm responsible for all the lives in the York Shrine church. I hope you can understand," says Father.

Sandra looks down. After a long pause, she wipes her tears off her cheeks, closes her eyes and takes a breath, and says, "Yes, Father."

Chapter 3

The Flashback

Sandra speaks…

Well, it's quite a horrible story. I want to be candid and tell you everything in detail. I want to talk about the things that have been buried in my heart for many years. I had neither attempted to share with anyone nor did I forget. Witnessing or experiencing an abusive relationship is one of the cruelest things for any child to endure during their childhood days. I spent days seeing my mom's pain. I was a bystander of both physical and emotional events. My mom was a fundamentalist, so she believed everything would turn out to be good one day. None of our friends or relatives knew about the abuse because my father would portray it as if he treated us well and we were the ideal family on earth. My mom, Sarah, never used to complain about him to anyone other than God. My mom and I always appreciated our time together; I had grown up listening to bible stories. She was an excellent storyteller. I can still hear her voice when I sleep as if she's lying beside me and narrating the stories. I admired my mom a lot. She worked in a bible school; she was an organized and dedicated worker.

My dad, Daniel, often got home drunk. I used to be scared to death to see him that way. I never wanted my mom to get hurt. I always told her to be quiet, no matter what happened, especially at the dinner table. Whenever we had dinner together, he would start an unwanted argument, and my mom's eyes would turn red and wide with fear. Sometimes, it would end up just as an argument, but she would also get beaten up if my dad was too drunk. It was hard for her to talk to others about what she was going through in her life. She lived with the hope that, eventually, he'd be a good man.

On a bitterly cold Monday, it was about 8.15 in the morning. My mom dropped me off at school and left for work. Usually, she used to pick me up from school, but whenever she was busy, her friend Ms. Barbara, who was also a parent of my classmate, would drop me home. Unexpectedly, the school got canceled on that day, and the principal announced to all the children to go home. My mom couldn't come, so she asked Ms. Barbara to drop me by. She was one of my mom's good friends those days. At 11.30 in the morning, she dropped me off at home. I asked her to have a cup of coffee, but she refused my invitation as she had important work to attend to. So, we waved hands at each other. Like every other day, I casually went into my house, but I saw a pair of cowboy boots in our shoe rack, which I hadn't seen before. My dad never used to wear them, either. The room was filled with smoke. It smelled weird, and I didn't know it was marijuana. My own nearly infallible instincts alerted me that something was terribly wrong.

I was really afraid to get into my own house. As I tiptoed to enter the room, my dad could barely recognize me because he was high on drugs, resting himself on the couch, and didn't know what was happening around him. There was another man in his early forties sitting opposite my dad, who had a bottle of whiskey in his hand. He looked at me in a glace from head to toe. I had never seen him before with my dad, and I was sure that he wasn't his friend and wondered how he panned out bringing him home. I was afraid of standing there. He got up, threw the bottle away, and came toward me. I was shivering and didn't know what to do. He unbuttoned his shirt and pant. As he approached me, he got completely naked. I felt cold chills run down my spine. I cried, "Daddy, daddy," many times out loud. Unfortunately, he couldn't hear me, so I ran into the bedroom. The door was wide open, and he was hell on wheels and grabbed my hair. "Just do what I say. It won't take that long. You won't get hurt," he whispered into my ears. I cried and begged him to leave me alone, but nothing went into that demon's ear. Providentially, there was a baseball bat to my reach. I took it with no time and bludgeoned him badly. He became infuriated, clenched both of his fists tightly, and gnashed his teeth wildly. I thought, "That's it. He's going to kill me," but in my favor, I saw a pistol in my dad's jacket. I sprinted to the gun promptly, grabbed it, and held it against him. I said, "If you move an inch toward me, you will be dead." That was the first time I saw a man's fear. He was frightened and didn't dare to take any steps further.

> *"Defeat is not a result of failure but a state of being dastard. One's ineptitude can quickly get one trapped in any adversity, but it takes a lot of courage to deal with it. Remember, you've already lost if you don't try, but the satisfaction of your battle will be a reward, whether or not you succeed."*

Well, I'm not the kind of person who'd get stuck in a situation, but I'm rather a person who'd give it my best shot and try to come out of it. He got his hands up in the air, walked out of the room, grabbed his clothes, and disappeared. Right after that, my dad got up and was astonished to see me standing and pointing the gun at him. He was scared too. I dropped the gun immediately on the floor and said, "No, dad, I used it to protect myself…that man tried to…" He slapped in my face twice very badly and asked, "Where's my friend? What did you do? Did you kill him?" I replied, "No dad, I didn't kill him. He ran away." My dad didn't have any patience to listen to me.

He was under the influence of drugs and staggered as he walked toward me. I was petrified to look at him and wanted to go to my room, but he grabbed me by my hand, slapped me again, and asked, "Why didn't you go to school today? Where were you roaming? I didn't expect you home." He was so mad at me and took a baseball bat to swing on my face. He was not in his control. I was stunned and had no clue what to do. There was a glass of water next to me. I splashed it on his face and pushed him onto the couch. Hence, he dropped the bat and fell down.

The situation had worsened, and my action had added more fuel to the fire. I actually wanted to run away from the house, but I stayed there because I didn't want to leave my mom alone with my father. I was the only person she could trust and depend on in the entire world. He slowly got up on his foot, came closer to me, held me by my hair, and said, "You dare not say anything to anybody, including your mother. If you make an attempt to tell anyone that I brought a stranger home and had marijuana, I won't hesitate to burn both of you alive."

I was absolutely terrified, and my cheek had an impression of his five fingers. I could barely speak a word; I just nodded my head promptly and went straight to my room. My mom got home late that day, and I had gone to bed a little early. Usually, I'd wait for her, and we would have dinner together, but that day I had to cover up everything.

Although my mom tried to wake me up, I told her I already had dinner. "You please eat and go to sleep, mom." I said, "Good night, and love you, mom," with tears sliding out of my eyes. My mom had walked in, seen my leg, and quietly patched me up, believing I was sound asleep. The following day, I physically felt better but avoided having a face-to-face conversation with my mom to hide my dad's fingerprints on my cheeks.

Days passed. I noticed a lot of changes in my dad's behavior. There were no arguments and no abusive words. He was rarely drunk. But he was always on his cell phone, and there were nights when he never came home. Neither of us had the guts to ask what was going on with him, but I was inquisitive to know about it.

I wanted to see what he's got in his black suitcase, which he often carried with him. I waited for the right opportunity to check it out but did not dare to touch it. One day, accidentally, it was left open on the table in his bedroom while he was having a conversation with someone on the porch.

I casually got in to find out what was there in the suitcase. It was right next to me on the table. Suddenly, I heard a rough voice. "What are you doing here?" "Oh, sorry, dad, I was just searching for my cellphone." I said.

I didn't even look at his face and got out of his room as fast as I could. If I don't do what I wanted to do, I'll become restless, and so I was. My mom noticed it and asked me, "What are you wondering about?" I said, "Nothing, mom," and sank down quietly on the couch next to her.

He came down the stairs in a suit and a tie. It was a vivid red Hermes tie that my mom had bought him on a trip to Berlin. He looked terrific. Both my mom and I were so glad to see him in a tuxedo after a very long time. He came straight to me and blew a kiss on my forehead. He held my mom in his hand and kissed her gently. "I apologize for everything I did; I know that both of you had gone through a lot of pain, and it's not fair to expect your forgiveness in an instant. But let me tell you something; things are gonna get better for us."

We were absolutely speechless to hear him saying those words. I remember how my dad used to tuck me into bed and read me my bedtime stories. He used to pick me up from school every day and take me to the park. I had a great time with him before my grandfather Antonio passed away.

He told my mom, "I'm heading north for a business meeting; I hope everything will turn out well as I expect. Please pack things up and we are leaving tonight. We're moving to Rockville, which is about 1,400 miles away from here. We are going to start a new life there." We neither denied the idea nor did we accept it.

My mom and I couldn't believe what was happening around us, but we were certainly happier than ever before. She was right. She always told me, "Hold on to your faith and never let it go. Things will turn out to be good one day." God had answered all of her prayers; my mom immediately took me to the altar and thanked God for having changed my father to be a better person again. She was always grateful to God. As my dad said, we packed our luggage and were ready to leave as soon as he came.

* * *

While Sarah and Sandra were waiting, Daniel was on his way up north, listening to loud music in his car. He was thinking about his father and how he had gotten into the diamond business. His father, Antonio, had direct contact with people in Kimberly, South Africa, and Freetown, Sierra Leone. He was mainly into illegal trade, shady dealings, and making money from smuggled and conflict diamonds.

Daniel got a pretty good hand over his dad Antonio's underground business. His father was born in Rome, where Carnevale di Venezia was very famous. He was fascinated by it and had never missed even a year of participating. His father took him there, but he didn't show any interest because he was not comfortable in the elaborate costume. Somehow, he tried to indulge himself voluntarily to make his father happy and dressed up as 'Medico Della Peste' with its long beak; it's one of the most strange and recognizable Venetian masks. The mask is often white, consisting of a hollow beak, round eyeholes, and crystal discs, creating a bespectacled effect.

That event was exclusively for big shots and rich diamond merchants around the world. Antonio was certainly not convinced to see his son dressed up like that, and he wanted him to wear the Louis XV costume, which was much more decorative. People were having fun as the celebration started. There was a woman dancing next to Daniel. "Wow, what a wonderful move! There must be a beautiful face hidden behind the mask," he said.

She turned and looked at him sharply. "Oh, I mean, your dancing moves are great." She was wearing Moretta, a small strapless black velvet oval mask with wide eyeholes; it was large enough to conceal a woman's identity. Both of them were not interested in taking part in that event which clearly showed the type of costume they chose. She got a pass to this event from one of her friends, who was a tycoon. She was inexorable and obligated to participate in the event. At times, accidental incidents or uncertain decisions will decide the rest of the journey of our lives. Although she was unable to speak with the mask on, she managed to answer his question.

Daniel was a brave and handsome man who could easily attract any woman in a matter of seconds; he called her for a date right away at LaMatriciana.

He couldn't wait any longer to meet her and reserved a perfect table just for the two of them by the window, holding a red rose in his hand to impress her. He turned and found himself gazing at a gorgeous woman who looked fashionable in her petite ruffled, high-low gown dress. They had more common thoughts, ideas, and interests and had a great time together. The first date had gone well, and it stayed fresh in their minds. After a few dates, they both fell in love.

Daniel revealed his intention to his father that he wanted to marry her. "What's her name?" His father asked. "Her name is Sarah, and she is the most beautiful woman I've ever met," said Daniel. Sarah was indeed an intelligent and gorgeous woman; Antonio couldn't find any reason to deny her. They were married and started their lives with lots of love; Sarah didn't like Daniel doing business with his father as it was illegal and dangerous. She told him not to get involved and to stay away from it.

She was a dedicated and the most profound Christian in town; she was a regular church-goer. Daniel trusted her in everything and never had a difference of opinion with her. He started to detach himself from his father's business gradually. After a year, they were blessed with a beautiful baby girl and named her 'Sandra Jones.'

They rarely visited Antonio; Sarah often avowed Daniel to be dropped out completely, not just for himself but for the goodness of the family too. Sarah's constant pursuit and the responsibility of being a father have superseded Daniel's interest and involvement in the illegal business; he promised his wife that he won't get involved in it anymore. And as said, he avoided meeting people, deleted his contacts to ignore unnecessary phone calls, and completely disconnected himself from the gray market. That was his father's intention, too, so he didn't disturb him either.

Daniel was a devoted family man who would sacrifice anything for Sarah and Sandra. When they were ill, he took them to the hospital. They always had dinner together. He constantly looked out for the well-being and safety of his family. To him, they were everything. Years passed by, Antonio got older and knew that without his son's help, it'd be challenging to survive in this business because it was not easy to trust anybody. He had many foes in the industry, and all of them were waiting for the right time to take him down.

One day, Antonio was severely attacked in an ambush for possessing six valuable diamonds, but he absquatulated them and reached Daniel's house's backyard. He had a shot in his right chest, bleeding through his nose and blood all over his head. He was holding his breath to see his beloved son. Daniel was totally shattered to see his father dying and wanted to take him to the hospital, but Antonio refused and said, "It's all over. Please, don't try to save me. I got to go." He handed Daniel a small velvet sack with six first-quality diamonds worth about half a billion dollars. "I know Sarah doesn't like it, and I don't want this to go to anybody other than you. Please don't say no; keep it." He stuffed the diamonds in his hands and closed his eyes forever. After acquiring such valuable paragons in hand, Daniel thought it was not a good idea to be here, not because he was afraid of Ricardo but for the promise he made to his wife Sarah and for the sake of his family too. So, he moved to Huntington.

Antonio had raised Daniel on his own as his wife had passed away at an early age. He taught Daniel how to swim, drive a car, and the tricks of the diamond trade. He was like a friend to him, more than a father figure. Daniel became an alcoholic to forget the loss of his beloved father and started hating everyone, including Sarah and his daughter. He blamed himself for his father's death. Sarah strongly believed that her husband was not a born perpetrator, and there were a lot of good qualities in him that she believed would come out again, so she constantly prayed about it.

Now, Daniel realized how cruel it was to hurt his own family. He wanted to sell all the diamonds that he got from his father, move to a new place, and start afresh.

* * *

Daniel turned the music down in the car to answer a phone call from one of his partners. "Hey Martin, I'll be there in an hour," said Daniel.

"Hold on, the meeting spot has changed, and you need to come to Mulberry Island, which is roughly about 75 miles from Thermopolis," said Martin.

Daniel and Martin had been friends since high school. Martin Joined the business after Daniel quit. And Daniel hadn't been in touch with him for many years so he didn't know whether he was still his friend or working for someone else and plotting against him. He was unhappy about the sudden change of plan because it had been many years since he had left the business, so he couldn't guess what was happening and had no idea about the new people who had emerged in the market. He wasn't even in a position to withdraw now, as he needed Martin's help to sell the diamonds. Thus, he had to take a chance. He was a very confident and stern man who took calculated risks, which was one of the reasons his father, Antonio, had always taken him to all the important business deals.

The change of location of the rendezvous at the last minute is iterating in Daniel's mind. Finally, he reached his destination. An island was seen far off, which was about two and a half kilometers away from the shore. He could barely see anything as it was dark and foggy. There was another car parked far from the shore; it was a four-seated white Ford Mondeo Fusion.

Daniel had distinct enthrallment on the spot, closely paying attention to every detail around him. He clearly knew the atmosphere of the business, and there was no way that it could change over the decade. His instinct alerted him that something was fishy. He bravely walked to the fifteen-foot-long jetty and spotted a small-sized motorboat docked at the very end of it. He called Martin as he got on the wooden passage and said the location seemed more suspicious, but Martin convinced him as it was too risky to handle such a lot of money in a commonplace. "If the cops get hold of us, then nobody can even see a penny, and we will spend the rest of our lives in prison," said Martin. But Daniel was not fully convinced that it was the right location to do such a big transaction. He checked his gun to make sure it was fully loaded, carefully undocked the boat, and headed toward the island. He could see some lights lit in the lonely cottage. His uncertainty had exponentially increased as he got closer and closer. At the same time, his attitude didn't allow him to back off either.

As he reached the shore, two men were standing there to receive him at gunpoint. Daniel was not shocked because he had already expected that. He asked, "Why are you pointing the gun at me? I have just come by myself, as you can see." "We know what we are doing. Now, give me the suitcase; otherwise, I will blow your head off," said Ron. They took him to the cottage. There he was, Ricardo, in his tuxedo, sitting in an armchair with his legs crossed and holding a Cuban cigar. Martin was standing next to him with an MK-18 mod 1.

For many years, Ricardo was Antonio's business partner, but they fell out due to some misunderstanding. Daniel also knew that Ricardo was the one who killed his father in the reprisals of the business adversaries, but he didn't expect him to be there at this spot.

Ricardo was aware that the diamonds were in Daniel's custody. He had known him since the beginning of his carrier. Because Daniel had made a significant contribution to both Antonio and Ricardo's success and no one ever dared to mess up with him. Ricardo was quite sure that it was impossible to seize the diamond from Danial's hand, so he tricked him by using Martin as bait.

Daniel was very calm and composed in spite of what was happening around him. "Why am I at gunpoint? What do you intend to do?" asked Daniel. "Where are those diamonds? Hand them over to me and get lost," said Ricardo with a cigar in his mouth. "You know very well that I quit before my father's death. I got no diamonds, no money, and no nothing. Just let me go," cried Daniel. Ricardo glanced at Shawn, one of the bodyguards. He suddenly hit Daniel in the back of his head; he instantly collapsed and became unconscious.

Meanwhile, they broke open the suitcase and took the diamonds, which were carefully kept in a small red velvet sack. After a while, Daniel slowly regained consciousness, tried to get on his feet, and vigilantly inspected if anyone was around, but there was no sign of anybody. He took the boat immediately to leave the spot as soon as possible.

* * *

Sandra continues…

Mom had concocted a big dinner likely to appeal to my dad; she cooked all of my dad's favorite food: cobb salad, pot roast, chicken fried steak, baked beans, a full turkey, and raspberry tart for dessert. That was the first time I'd ever seen my mom literally beaming with happiness. We were waiting for my dad at the dinner table. We phoned him many times but got no answer. Mom spent the entire night waiting for him on the porch despite the freezing cold.

She was worried about him and didn't have dinner. It was about 3 o'clock in the early morning; I called her to go to bed. She kept staring at the gate, waiting for him badly. I turned off all the lights and went to bed with mom. She never slept a wink; suddenly, I heard my dad's car sound. "Mom, dad's home," I cried. We jumped out of bed expeditiously; I ran to open the door.

I couldn't believe what I saw. We were devastated; he fell down from the car onto the floor as I opened the door. His white shirt under the coat was fully red, and the tie that my mom had gifted him was dripping blood. I took the phone to call 911, but he snatched it from me and said, "Don't call anybody." Dad asked me to take a small sack from his jacket and said, "Those are the most expensive diamonds in the entire world; I inherited them from my dad, and now I'm giving them to you. I was tricked by my ex-friend Martin. They trapped me in a bogus business deal to steal the gems from me, but I anticipated everything beforehand, so I made six fake diamonds and kept them in my suitcase. They thought those were real and missed the original ones which were hidden in my jacket. If they ever find them fake, they will track you down and kill you all."

With a heavy heart and stammering even to utter a word, my mom asked him, "Who shot you? What happened?"

"After I tricked them with the duplicate diamonds, I thought everything was over. I checked the room. Nobody was there. I believed that they took the stones and left. So, I took the motorboat to leave the place, but suddenly, there were four gunshots echoing across the island. Two were missed, but one of them got through my right shoulder, and the other one hit my back. I knew that Ricardo wouldn't leave me alive, and

I sensed they were far behind me, looking through the binoculars to make sure I was down. I pretended to be dead and somehow managed to reach the shore. The upper part of my body was fully drenched in blood, but I didn't die, and I didn't want to die. I wanted to see you and my little princess. I wanted to see my family before I died. I gathered my strength, hobbled to the car, and drove very fast. I was unable to breathe. My eyes were blurry, and my pulse was dropping. Yet I drove continuously, without a halt. Luckily, I'm here with you, my love," said Daniel.

Dad gave us a piece of paper with the address of the house in Rockville and told mom, "I'm sorry for leaving you so early, my dear. Stay safe. Take care of our daughter. Love you." He succumbed to his last breath and died. Death is a natural and inevitable part of everyone's life, but to be killed for mere possession is a grievance, and the pain of seeing a loved one dying in our arms is unbearably hurtful. Although he failed to show his real love after the demise of my grandfather, his parting moments portrayed how desperately he wanted to protect us. Betrayed, being shot with blood oozing out and dropping pulse, he was adamantly holding on to his life to see his beloved wife and daughter, which showed how truly my father loved us. I cannot forget how his eyes looked at us before he closed them forever.

* * *

"The memory of a person will reverberate when there is an absence of the physical body of whom we have the reminiscence. Nostalgic agony can be severe when consciousness witnesses that your loved one is extinct. The probability of getting retarded is higher if one doesn't let time do its business, as it's the best medicine."

Sarah's and Sandra's most sweet memories of Daniel had become a torment to their present moment as they loved him even after he was tarnished in character.

* * *

Shocking and surrounded by a pool of blood, my mom couldn't stop crying, and her face was swollen very badly. We felt like our entire world had shattered into pieces. We didn't want to waste even a minute. So, we put my dad in the car and headed to Bowersville, which was 320 miles away from where we were located. Mom wanted to interment my dad there as it was his favorite place. In her whole married life, she went there only twice with my dad as it was a secret place for my grandpa and him.

My mom drove the car, and the only way that connected the location was a narrow bridge; it would take just one car at a time. We reached there at 6 o'clock in the early morning. The place was so quiet, and nobody was there other than us, completely isolated from the rest of the world. We buried him in the backyard. I placed freshly plucked wildflowers, a roughly made cross. Mom recited a Psalm. Everything was done perfectly, and my dad rested peacefully in his untold place. Scrubs and tall weeds covered almost all the areas around the house, which clearly showed that no one had been there for years; hence, there was no path, and it was unkempt.

My mom didn't show any interest in getting inside the house, but I wanted to see what it would look like. Luckily, she had the keys, unlocked the rusty knob, and slammed open the door. She told me how she spent her day with my dad in that house; there were many secret rooms that nobody could find. Mom didn't want to keep the diamonds with her and didn't dare to sell them in the market, so she decided to hide it in the secret house, which made sense to me too.

Chapter 4

At Rockville

After the sepulture, Sarah didn't want to spend any more time at Bowersville, so they immediately continued their journey to the address that Daniel gave them. After hours of driving, they reached the most beautiful place on earth, Rockville. The morning stars peeped down like silver asters, glinting and shimmering. Everything looked so wonderful. Unfortunately, they balked at admiring Mother Nature as they had just lost their beloved family member. Sandra notices the name board "Sarah's Ville" She calls out to her mom, "Mom, look there, that's our house; see, your name is on it." This is the kind of house that Sarah always wanted to live in with her family. It was situated on the outskirt of the village, and there were a few neighboring houses separated by long pathways, shrubs, and bushes. It was a cozy and comfortable house for just two people. There was a spacious living room on the ground floor and a large window with a spectacular view of the field. On the same floor, there were two bedrooms, a modern kitchen room, and two bathrooms. And on the second floor, there was a study room and a room for a large snooker board which they never used. On top, there was an attic which was really magnificent for being with friends, but they never had any friends except Debbie and her kids Simon and Cathy. Finally, a patio with a wooden table and four chairs was perfect for having coffee and breakfast. It clearly shows how much Daniel loved his family, but he was not lucky enough to be with them.

Sarah didn't expect her daughter to get freshened up so early and kept the breakfast ready on the table; they sat together, held hands, and prayed for the peace of Daniel. She then handed the newspaper to her mother and poured coffee into the cup. Also, pancakes and maple syrup were served. After breakfast, they went out to explore the place; it was a small village with just a few people and old horse chariots, but there was a decently developed town situated about five kilometers from Sarah's Ville. Everything was there: hospitals, schools, restaurants, supermarkets, and shopping malls. They bought some stuff that was necessary for them to start a new life.

Sarah got a job at The Faith Baptist Bible School, where Sandra continued her high school too. It was more convenient for them to be together in the same place. They used to go and come together in the morning as well as in the evening. She was a clever girl and always off the charts. Sarah wanted her daughter to matriculate to Harvard, but it was far away from

Rockville; Sandra never liked the idea of leaving her mother alone to pursue her degree. Both of them had purposely avoided their neighbors in Rockville because they didn't want to harbor any inquisitive people. They also avoided community gatherings, weddings, Thanksgiving, Christmas, and New year celebrations to stay away from unnecessary problems. The only place they went, other than their work, was the Church on Sundays. But there was one woman called Debbie, who worked with Sarah in the same school. She had been inviting them for lunch for a very long time. Alas, they accepted her invitation and decided to go as she was a single mom too.

Debbie was a kind woman who lived just fifteen minutes away from school in town and had two kids, Cathy and Simon. Her husband passed away when her second child was just two years old. Sarah inspired her a lot. Raising children as a single mother was not easy, and she did that very well. They were all having lunch at the dining table; Debbie asked Sandra, "What would you like to do after graduating from high school?" "I want to do economics at the New Mission University here in Rockville because I don't want to leave my mom," said Sandra. Debbie was so proud of her and appreciated her decision. They all spent their evening together and had a nice time.

Usually, Sarah and Sandra used to go shopping on alternate Sundays of every month. Likewise, one Sunday, they went to a small shopping mall where Sarah saw one of Daniel's old friends; she was shocked, clung to Sandra's hand, and dragged her to the car. "Mom, what are you doing? We haven't bought anything yet," said Sandra. "Be quiet. We got to go. I'll tell you everything in the car." She didn't want to be identified by any of her husband's friends. It's been three years since they moved to Rockville, and that was the first time she encountered a person who was associated with her husband back in Huntington.

Sandra successfully graduated from high school and got admission to a college of her choice in the exact stream she wished for, as she was one of the school toppers in the academic year. After years of isolation from people, Sarah decided to break the chain for a while to celebrate her daughter's success. A small party was organized in honor of Sandra's achievement. Only a few people were invited, including Debbie's family and some of Sandra's high school friends. Even though there were people around wishing and celebrating Sandra's success, she still missed her father's presence at the graduation ceremony because a father figure is irreplaceable. She tried to hide her sadness behind her smile as she thought it would bring a domino effect to her mother's smile, and Sarah felt the same. She kept it together for her child's sake. Life was smooth, and everything went well.

"Mom, do you think we need to go to Bowersville to check if those diamonds are safe?" asked Sandra.

"No, we are not going anywhere. You don't worry about them," said Sarah coldly.

Sandra also wanted to see her old house to know if someone had checked in, searching for the diamonds, but her mother never encouraged such a thought.

During the summer vacation of her final year at the university, she was hunting for a part-time job to help her mother with some extra money. She finally found one in The Daily Mail newspaper, jotted down the phone number, and dialed it immediately.

The phone rings.

"Hello, may I speak with Mr. Phil Harrison?" said Sandra.

"Yes, speaking," said Phil.

"I saw your advertisement in The Daily Mail newspaper, and I'm sure I'll be the right candidate for your requirements," said Sandra.

"Why don't you meet me in person? I hope you got my address as well," said Phil. Sandra said she was very interested in meeting him and hung up the call.

She was very excited after having the conversation with Phil and couldn't wait to tell Sarah about her part-time job idea. "Mom, there's an opening for a part-time job in Stans Avenue. I just spoke with a person called Phil, and he asked me to meet him tomorrow.

I guess I almost got the job," said Sandra excitedly. But Sarah didn't look delighted. "I know what's going on in your mind, mom. It's okay. Let's be positive."

Sandra took her bike to go to Phil's house as it was only 5 kilometers from her place. She parked her bike by the tree and stood in front of the huge iron gate. With a security check on the left, the man in the livery inquired to her politely, "Hello, miss, who are you looking for?" "I've come here for a job interview and would like to meet Mr. Phil." He called Phil to get a confirmation and sent her in.

Sandra was awestruck to see such a beautiful and luxurious house. It looked palatial; it was the biggest house she had ever seen. It has a dark brown roof, beige walls, and a huge corridor with yellow and blue focus lights on the ceiling. There were three expensive cars parked in the garage. She thought he must be the richest man in town. The house was surrounded by spectacular greenery, and many rose plants were on both sides of the patio. She was so happy to be there.

Doorbell rings.

A man in his late fifties came out; he had a long, lush salt pepper hair tint and stood 6.2 feet tall, with sparkling blue eyes. He escorted her to sit on a red chair by the garden pond. They both sat opposite each other; Phil asked some personal questions to get to know more about Sandra, but she dodged them wisely to avoid revealing any information about her father and her previous life back in Huntington.

"This job involves a lot of physical work, such as watering the plants, mowing the lawn, and maintaining the garden. Do you think you'll be able to do all that?" asked Phil.

"Of course I can," said Sandra enthusiastically.

"All right, the working hours are from Monday to Saturday, 9 am to 1 pm or from 2 pm to 6 pm. You may choose one of the slots that suit you at your convenience. You will be paid $30.00 per hour for the first three weeks. Upon finishing your probation period, you will get $40.00 per hour. If you agree, meet me here at 9 am sharp tomorrow," said Phil.

Sandra went home happily and told her mother that she got through the interview, what she would be paid for, and when she would be starting her work. The next day, she was there at Phil's house sharply at 9 o'clock, waiting for him to give instructions. He didn't come out; after a while, she phoned him, but it was switched off. There was a speaker and a calling bell on the door. She pressed it gently and heard a voice, "Hey, Sandra. I'm busy right now. You may water the plants and hang out in the garden. Leave sharply at 1 o'clock." She did what was instructed and left exactly at 1 pm.

"How was your first day at work?" asked Sarah.

"Fantastic, mom! In fact, I expected a lot of work, but I just watered the plants and watched birds," said Sandra joyfully, but as a doting mother, Sarah's fear and suspicion grew stronger because she was paid $30 dollars per hour, which was a lot of money for just menial work. However, she did not let her daughter know the thought that was lingering in her mind, as it would pull her down. Sandra takes after her father in taking risks, and that's one of the reasons why Sarah was worried the most.

Sandra was so punctual and regular to work. Her daily routine at work was watering the garden, trimming the trees and shrubs, fertilizing, and mowing the lawn. On the last day of her probation period, she was called into the house where Phil was comfortably sitting on a couch, offered a seat to Sandra, and asked her if she wanted to have a tour of his house. She accepted it politely and also asked him if she was the only person he had hired. He said that she was the only person for now, but there would be more down the line. The hallway flows into a large, wide staircase; he took her to the second floor of the house, where many types of wallpapers and pictures of nude girls and women displayed on the wall and showcased on the tables and shelves. She felt so embarrassed to be in that place. "I'm a photographer. Please, don't judge me on this," said Phil jubilantly. Sandra looked puzzled and asked, "Are you the only one who lives in this big house?" He said, "Yes." He didn't give any more details for that question and took a few snaps of Sandra on his camera without getting her permission.

"Everyone has the right to question if pictures or videos are taken without consent because they can be misused easily in this digital world."

Sandra got so mad at what he had just done. He immediately took his laptop and transferred the pictures. "Don't worry. I just take pictures of whoever I meet because that's what my profession is," said Phil. She looked around the house. There were some magazines and albums with a lot of obscene pictures, and there was a pen drive on the table next to his laptop. Initially, she wanted to check what was there on his laptop, but it was quite risky to do so, as it was her first day in the house. She decided to take it slow but purloined the pen drive as it was handy. She was very confident because she knew there was no CCTV camera in the room.

As soon as she got home, without even changing her dress and having lunch, she immediately connected the pen drive to her laptop and found a lot of pornographic videos. Those were definitely not common videos people download from the internet, but they looked like the videos were directed and shot live. Because all of the videos were long and not edited. What was really heartbreaking to Sandra was that most of them were children. She was also worried whether he had targeted her and had decided to push her into the smut industry.

She browsed the internet to know more about the sex traffickers and found shocking information, "The FBI estimates sex trafficking in the U.S. involves 100,000 children. 60% of child sex trafficking victims recovered through FBI raids across the U.S. in 2013 were from foster care or group homes." (*Source: National Foster Youth Institute*)

Just like her father in character, Sandra was a fearless and confident girl who never bothered about the consequences. She wanted to gather more evidence to catch Phil red-handed.

The phone rings.

"Hey, Sandra. Good morning! From today onwards, you won't be working outside the garden. I need your help to set things up inside the house," said Phil.

Sandra had already anticipated it. She wanted to gather some documents to get him prosecuted, so the request was accepted. She didn't tell anything to her mother but wanted to handle it all by herself, because she clearly knew that her mother would never let her get involved in this. She was well-prepared and reached his house sharply at 9 am. Usually, underprivileged women or children of single parents, foster children, and homeless women are the most vulnerable targets for sex traffickers. Phil knew that Sandra was a child of a single mom, who was under economic constraint, so he was trying to take advantage of her situation. He gave her a stack of photographs of nude children. Some of them were pornographic; he wanted to make her get used to them.

"Why are you handing them over to me? What am I supposed to do with them?" asked Sandra defiantly.

"You are young and a beautiful kid; you'll have the most sophisticated life that you can ever imagine if you just do what I say," said Phil.

She neither refused nor acceded, though she was a bundle of nerves at that moment, yet the urge to get him arraigned had motivated her to take it as a challenge. "You may take your own time, but remember, this is the most unprecedented opportunity to make a fortune out of your beauty," said Phil. Accidentally, she overheard his conversation with his partners: "If she doesn't agree with the proposal, give her chloroform and transport her to another state. She would never know where she was." But she never got daunted by any of it. There was a file in his reading room that seemed more important, she wanted to see what it was, but the man was sticking around. Favorably, a phone call dragged him to the ground floor, which gave her more time to pore over it. She was peeping at the staircase to make sure he wasn't coming back and running her eyes over the document carefully.

She utilized the opportunity wisely, used her cell phone, and took pictures of all the important items.

She was astounded to know that the group which Phil was associated with had exploited thousands of children and forced them into prostitution.

"A 2013 report by the HHS Administration on Children, Youth and Families cited a number of alarming statistics, including several studies showing that fifty to more than ninety percent of children who were victims of child sex trafficking had been involved with child welfare services (HHS, ACF, 2013)".

She could not take the file out of the house, so she thought the picture on her cellphone would be good for now. Suddenly, she heard an indistinct sound of footsteps; she didn't want to take any risks, thereby she immediately put everything back in place.

The next day, she brought a bag with her to take the albums and all the other important hard discs, files, and documents. He noticed her carrying a bag she had never brought before, raising his suspicion. He had been keeping an eye on her throughout the day.

"I have arranged your room completely. I'll take leave now. See you tomorrow," said Sandra hesitantly.

She was grabbed by her hand and pulled toward him. He put his arm around her and asked, "Are you ready today?" She was trembling with fear and said, "I can't do it today. Please give me some time." She took the information about many children, a hard disc, and the file in her bag. She became anxious and restless; she wanted to leave the place before getting caught.

"Phil, I just got a phone call from my mom. She is not well. I need to leave now. I will extend my work till 3 o'clock tomorrow," said Sandra nervously.

"Of course, you can, but I want to know something before you leave. How come your bag is so heavy all of a sudden, as if you have a hippo in it?" said Phil sarcastically.

The ticking sound of seconds on the clock was so audible as the room was filled with the silence of fear and anger. Phil's face had turned red in outrage as he got closer. Sandra was shaking from head to toe and dropped her bag in fright. Phil took her bag, tore it open, and found many of his documents, his laptop, and pornographic pictures of the children. He was gasping for his breath in wrath. He slapped her face, pushed her into the corner of the room, and took a whip to whack her off. She started telling his name and address with landmarks and cried, "Don't kill me. Don't kill," so loudly. He stood perplexed and looked at the whip and her face, getting puzzled by her reaction. The cops arrived within a fraction of a second. Sandra had cleverly dialed 911. While the caller was on the line, she gave her all the information. The police shackled and dragged him to the van; later, the FBI traced the entire network of sex traffickers and saved thousands of children and women from them.

Sandra became the headline in all the newspapers, and the news got sensational across the nation. A few reporters had come to Sarah's Ville to interview her, but Sarah didn't allow anybody. She wanted to protect her daughter's identity not only from the smugglers who had killed her husband brutally but also from the sex traffickers too. It would definitely bring the killers home if there is any clue of their whereabouts. Everyone in town appreciated Sandra for her bravery. Day by day, Sarah received more phone calls from all the news channels across the country. She explained to them very clearly, not to reveal her daughter's identity at any cost, as it would become a threat to her life. In today's world, nothing can be hidden for a long time because social media would definitely bring things into the limelight. Unfortunately, Some of the photos of Sandra and her current location were already leaked on social media and became viral. Millions of people had watched it, and so did Martin back in Huntington.

Chapter 5

From Huntington to Rockville

After Daniel was shot on the motorboat, he looked defunct through Ricardo's binoculars. But he still wanted to make sure that Daniel was dead.

Ricardo gave the binoculars to Martin and said, "Setting him free is like setting ourselves on fire, so see carefully if we had hit him well"

"Yes, Rick, he got the bullets on his back. He's down on the boat with blood all over his body. He should be dead. You can see it too" said Martin.

Ricardo got angry and smashed the binoculars against the wall and said, "I can't trust anything unless I physically see that by myself." Because Ricardo knew that Daniel's revenge could annihilate everybody, so they checked the entire island, but his corpse was not found. The ceded boat on the jetty, the missing car, and the trace of bloodstains on the shore had them speculate that he wasn't dead. Though letting him go was not a good idea, the priority of taking the gems into the market was high. So, they didn't want to hunt for him as the diamonds were already seized.

The despoiled diamonds were immediately taken to New York City for cutting and polishing, but they were found to be worthless duplicate stones. Ricardo became furious, and so did everyone; they never imagined that he would play a trick on them.

* * *

A couple of months before Daniel decided to team up with Martin to sell his diamonds, Martin found Daniel on Facebook and told him that he wanted to meet him in person. Daniel believed him a lot as they both were good friends in high school. Having gained his trust, Daniel invited him to his house for lunch and introduced him to his family members. Daniel told him about his father's demise, how heartbroken he was, and the fact that he did quite everything. Martin was never involved when Daniel was with his father in the business, so he took advantage of it and left no room for Daniel's suspicion. Martin told him that he had top reliable contacts in the market and tricked him into confessing that Daniel possessed his father's precious diamonds and got him inveigled in his plot. Martin pretended that he was in favor of him but schemed a vicious plan. He recommended selling his diamonds in the international market to make a huge amount of money. He professed to be a very nice guy who liked Daniel and his family a lot. He bought nice gifts for Sandra and talked with Sarah to know where she worked and who her friends were; basically, he gathered as much information as possible. Everything was a part of Ricardo's plan.

* * *

"I'd been to his house, and I know where it is. I know his wife, daughter, friends, and workplace. I know everything about them. Let's hit the road and get the diamonds back," said Martin coldly to Ricardo.

The door was locked, and the garage was empty. They shot open the lock of the front door and ransacked the entire house, but nothing was found. They immediately went to the school where Sarah worked, but it was closed. "Do you know if they have any close contacts in this neighborhood?" asked Ricardo. "Sarah has a friend called Barbara, who lives by Buckeye Lake. It's just about seven kilometers away from here. Perhaps she might have a clue about where they are." After a long search, they found her house and enquired about Sarah's family. The woman was terrified to see all four men, and one of them had a revolver. She said, "I've no idea where they live. My daughter said that Sandra hasn't come to school since August. I swear to God. I don't know anything about them." Ron gave her his phone number to send a message if she happened to know anything. They searched everywhere and traced all of their contacts but couldn't find them until that morning.

Martin was having his cup of coffee and casually browsing his cell phone when a notification popped up: "Sandra Jones, a young girl from Rockville, had caught a fifty-seven-year-old sex trafficker red-handed." He immediately recognized her and shared the link with the others. They were so happy to get a clue about them after so many years. "We need to handle this very carefully. First, we have to find out where they are, what they do, and whether Daniel is still alive," said Ricardo. Nobody knew what happened to Daniel or where did they go? "R-O-C-K-V-I-L-L-E," uttered Ricardo.

Sarah got a call from Debbie. "Hey, Sarah, why don't you stay with us for a while? Because it's not a good idea to be all by yourselves at times like this. They are a huge network of international sex traffickers; they might take vengeance on Sandra. What if she was targeted? Your lives are in jeopardy. Please come and stay with us here at my house just for a month or two. Once everything becomes normal, then you guys may go back home."

"You are so kind to care about us, and I'm glad that I got such a wonderful friend. I'm worried about your safety as well, and I don't want you guys to walk into any sort of trouble just because you're helping us," said Sarah.

Debbie convinced her to stay with them. Her younger son, Simon, was autistic. "We couldn't realize that there was something unusual with him until he was five years old, then we started paying attention to his behavior very closely." The first thing they noticed was that he had a lack of eye contact, repetitive behavior, and didn't eat or sleep properly. Eventually, he showed more symptoms of autism, such as delayed speech and usage of language skills, and gave unrelated answers to the questions asked. His name was on a waiting list of early development pediatricians in and around Ohio. She was told there would be a minimum of six months of waiting time, and he wasn't even eligible for the 'babies can't wait program.' Luckily, he got an appointment with a developmental pediatrician in just three months; the doctor diagnosed him with an autism spectrum disorder. "I took him for counseling and consulted psychologists but didn't find any remarkable improvement. The only thing that I could believe was my prayers; I've been praying every single day for the betterment of my son's mental health. I have also been taking him to the Church of Hope covenant ever since he was diagnosed with ASD. Trust me; there is an excellent improvement in his behavior now. My son is still an autistic child, but his condition is not as bad as how it used to be. I genuinely believe that it's all because of God's grace and I'm so grateful for that," said Debbie.

Debbie took them to the same church on Sunday morning; it was a big congregation in that locality, where many people gathered for a single service. Sandra became very popular after the incident, so every person in the church was able to recognize her.

They treated her as a real hero and appreciated her bravery as a young girl. She got so many invitations from a lot of people in the church for lunch and dinner; obviously, it was not possible to accept all, so she politely denied the requests from everyone.

Sandra grew fond of Simon; she used to take care of him as she would've cared for her brother if she had one. He never used to mingle with people so easily, because one of his conditions was having difficulties with social interaction. Her kindness and friendly nature had attracted him. He started liking her, and there was an excellent bond created between them. Sarah had nightmares and was often worried about her daughter's safety. She wished that she could talk to her old friend Barbara to find out what was going on in Huntington and also wanted to know if someone had visited her old house in search of the diamonds. But nothing gave her courage, so she remained concealed.

In another instance, when they were at the park, Cathy and Simon were playing with Sandra. Suddenly, Sarah grabbed her daughter's hand, dragged her to the car, and said, "We need to move from this place right now. I saw someone who looked like Martin behind the tree." Sandra shook her mother's hand and said, "You are always thinking about them, and that's the reason whomever you see, and whatever you see, everything looks like them. How long do you think we can run away like this? When can we live our lives normally like everyone else? Just forget it, mom. Relax." She took her mother to the tree and proved nobody was there.

Debbie bought a lovely dress for Sandra. Sarah was surprised and said, "Why are you doing all this?" It looks so expensive." It was a gift for her bravery, and she deserved it. They were asked to get dressed and be ready at 6 p.m. Sarah and her daughter didn't have a clue about what was happening.

Meanwhile, Ricardo planned to go to Rockville with the boys, but Martin stopped him. "You don't need to come, Ric. We can handle this. We'll get the diamonds and send you a message." All three men loaded their guns and started their journey. "Have you ever been there? Do you know where they live?" asked Shawn and Ron. Martin was driving the car and said, "Guys, listen, we don't know if Daniel is still alive, what they are doing there, and where their exact location is. I just saw them once, but I can vividly remember their faces. We'll have to search every nook and corner of Rockville to get hold of them." They stopped their car at a restaurant on the highway to have dinner; a driver got alighted from the vehicle with the name 'Rockville Village' written on his truck, which grabbed Martin's attention. He stopped the driver and asked if he was going to Rockville. The driver said, "Yes." He was heading back home.

"We are going to Rockville to see our cousin Sarah and her daughter Sandra; it's been more than five years since they moved there, and unfortunately, we've lost their contact information. Do you know anybody by those names who live there?" asked Martin.

The driver asked, "If they're your relatives, you should be able to know where they are. It's so weird that you don't even have their contact numbers. Where are you guys from, and how did you start your journey to find their whereabouts without having a single clue?" The driver refused to give them any information because he knew about Sarah and Sandra, as Sandra was the sensation of both local and national news. He suspected foul play, that they could be the sex traders tracking down Sandra to take revenge for ruining their flesh market empire.

Having no patience, Ron suddenly pointed his gun at the driver's back, pressed it so hard as if it could break his spine, and whispered into his ears, "Do you want to say where they are or die here right now?" With extreme trepidation, he said, "Yes, I heard about the girl, Sandra, and she helped the cops to catch a large network of sex traffickers. She became the talk of the town. To be honest with you guys, I don't know where they live, but I heard that her mother works at Faith Baptist church. Sandra completed high school there as well. Maybe you can go there and check them out. Please don't kill me." Everyone was glad about getting the vital information. As soon as they got the info, Martin snatched the gun from Ron and shot the driver right in his forehead, as he was impertinent to him initially.

Debbie took everybody in her car and never told anyone where she was taking them; Cathy was sitting in the front seat while the others were sitting at the back. Sarah asked her, "For Pete's sake, could you please tell us where we are going? Because I don't like suspense." Everyone in the car joined her. "Yes, we need to know where we are going." They were shouting and making noise in the car.

"Guys, I want everyone to be quiet and stop asking me any more questions. You all will know when we get there in another fifteen minutes," said Debbie.

As they reached the spot, Sandra was the first to get down. She looked ravishing in the red lace dress that Debbie had bought. The moon shone brightly, only to put her in the spotlight and showcase her natural beauty. Her hairdo added more grace, and she looked so beautiful as if a princess had arrived from the castle.

People were waiting at the reception with bouquets. Sarah and Sandra were amazed to see the crowd, and the giant welcome board read: "We proudly welcome the bravest girl of Ohio, Miss. Sandra Jones." They looked at Debbie and asked, "Why didn't you tell us anything about your idea?" She said, "Initially, I wanted to tell you everything, but I was afraid that you'd reject the whole idea in the name of safety.

I didn't want to get it sabotaged. Being a single mom, I can understand your concern that safety always comes first, but Sandra risked her life and saved thousands of children and women. What she did was truly remarkable! So, I spoke with the Father of this church; they organized a ceremony and invited the governor to preside over it." The chief guest appreciated her courage, awarded her medals, and told everyone to be as vigilant and responsible as Sandra.

After a long search, Martin, Shawn, and Ron had arrived at Schedel Gardens, where Sarah and Sandra were standing next to the governor with some cops around them. They were caught under the eagle eye of Martin. He discerned them in a matter of glimpse and told his buddies that the two women standing far off were Sarah and Sandra. It was impossible that they could get closer as there were cops around them. All three men had gotten back to their car to conspire on a perfect stratagem about how they could hook them and retrieve the diamonds. Among all three of them, Shawn was young, handsome, and charming. He had a touch of Brad Pitt about him; he could easily make any girl fall for him with his dashing personality and cosmic smile. Martin had chosen him to allure Sandra; he said, "Take a beautiful red rose from the garden. Give it to her and call her on a date." He waited for a good chance to propose to her. To his favor, she stepped away from the crowd to get some fresh air. He utilized this chance wisely, stood right behind her, and touched her ears with the rose petal. As she turned, he stood on one knee, extended the two-leafed rose, and said, "A flower for a flower." She was astounded and took a few moments to realize that she was not in the dreamland. There he was, still on his knee with the rose, "I will not get up until you take it." She immediately took it from him. She didn't ask who he was, where he was from, or what he wanted. He drew closer to her, looked into her eyes, and gave her a piece of paper with his phone number and the address to where he wanted to meet her the next time. She took the paper in her hand but didn't want to read it, nor did she throw it away.

Despite her slender outlook and cheerful character, nobody proposed to her, even in high school and university, because she had never given anyone such opportunities. Her mother nurtured her piously; she never wasted time hanging out with boys or other girls. She would mostly spend time with her mother in church. And her mother would always be around to make sure she was safe. That was the first time she had ever experienced that kind of feeling in her whole life; it was weird but unique, and she liked it. On the way back home, everyone in the car was listening to music and talking to each other about the party, but Sandra didn't say a word. She couldn't pay heed, although Simon was trying to grab her attention. She was completely lost. Debbie looked at her through the rear-view mirror and asked, "Honey, is everything alright?" She pretended as if nothing had happened but still couldn't resist thinking about him.

They reached home at 11.30 pm; everyone was fast asleep except Sandra. She reached for her pochette and drew out that small piece of paper that Shawn had given her. She was in a quandary about whether or not to open the paper; a series of thoughts had conflicted within herself, unable to handle the mixed feelings, yet her endearment had won. Finally, she carefully took out the paper and opened it with great curiosity: "I'd like to meet you tomorrow at 11 O'clock at the same spot where I gave you the rose. With love, Shawn Taylor." He also mentioned his WhatsApp number. She was not only nervous about meeting the handsome man again but afraid of falling in love with him too.

The next morning, she picked one of her favorite clothes from the closet; it was a plain blue bell-sleeve dress that gave the perfect contrast. She took her bike without telling her mom that she was going to meet a man who had given her a rose last night. "Someone's looking very happy and glittering. Is there anything special today?" asked Sarah. "No, mommy, just going to college; Bye, mom, love you," said Sandra and rode away. Sarah guessed there was something under wraps, but she didn't want to stress out her daughter. Shawn was sitting on the bonnet of his car, looking at the clear sky while hoping that she would come. He hopped off as she arrived and was glad that she showed up. He looked stunning to her, and she couldn't take her eyes off him. With a deceptive appearance, the beast was hidden behind his charisma. And her age had failed to notice the truth. Just like any other girl in their early twenties, she didn't ask anything about his personal life. They only had a general conversation about their likes and dislikes.

She was completely swept off her feet and was head over heels for him. Having been mesmerized by his sweet talk, she agreed to meet him again at one of the finest restaurants in town for an early dinner. Martin wanted to handle it differently; he instructed Shawn not to ask for any information about her past or personal life but to win her trust. Because he knows that Sandra is a clever girl, if he creates any room for speculation, she will be alerted and won't meet him again. To make her fall in love, get into her family, and become one of them sounds like a priority for Martin because he was aware of her influence on the local people and the police officers. Even though she liked him and went on a couple of secret dates, she was still a closed book to him. Her mother's concern about strangers had prevented her from bringing him home or introducing him to her.

"This is not gonna work. We can't wait anymore. Just make a plan, go to her house, and ask her at gunpoint," said Ron.

A new message popped up on her cell phone: "Hey, sweetheart! Whatcha doin'?" She responded, "Hey, there! Nothing much." During the chat, he casually asked her if she'd invite him to her house. "I'd love to! Actually, I was thinking about introducing you to my mom. Luckily, you asked me first," said Sandra cheerfully. That was exactly what he wanted to hear. She didn't want to take him to Debbie's house, so she decided to go back to Sarah's Ville with her mother. Simon was so attached to her. He didn't allow them to leave, but she promised to visit him every alternate day and take him to the park. "Why are you in such a hurry, honey? You still have another two weeks before your university reopens. Is there anything that you wanna do at home?" asked Sarah. "Let's go home, mom. I'll tell you everything there." She told her about Shawn right from the day she met him and the fact that he wanted to meet her mother. Sarah doesn't want her daughter to get hooked up with any random person because her intention was to find an orthodox and nice gentleman with Christian values through the church association. Initially, she didn't show any interest in meeting Shawn, but eventually, Sandra convinced her mother and got permission to invite him for lunch.

A new message was received: "Hey, Shawn! I just told my mom about you, and she's really excited to meet you."

In reality, Sarah agreed to meet him not because her daughter liked him a lot but because she wanted to see if he liked her from the bottom of his heart and would never cheat on her. On top of all, she wanted to ensure he was not after the diamonds. According to Sarah, Sandra may be brave but not clever enough to choose her right partner.

"If you could stop by for lunch, it would be much appreciated." Martin was so happy that she had taken the bait; this was the moment he'd been waiting for and gave Shawn an explicit instruction that no matter what happened, he should get into their house, point the gun right at their forehead, and ask where the diamonds were. He was happy and confident as everything was happening as per his plan. As Daniel's existence remained a question, Shawn was insisted on checking if there were just Sandra and her mother because Martin was afraid to face Daniel. "No, just my mom and I," replied Sandra. The car arrived at Sarah's Ville. Martin reiterated the plan to Shawn to make sure he executed it well.

"You go in first, have a chat with them, and ask where the diamonds are. If there is no response, send us a message. We'll be waiting in the car with the gun." Said Martin

Lunch was ready to be served. Only three of them were at the table. Sarah was sick, but despite that, she took her time and effort to prepare various delicious dishes for him.

Shawn was all set. He got his gun in his right sock to handle it at any time while Sandra was excitingly waiting to introduce him to her mother. "Mom, this is Shawn, and Shawn, this is my mom Sarah," said Sandra with a smile.. Food was placed neatly on the dining table, and three chairs were perfectly set around it. Sarah, Sandra, and Shawn sat triangularly. A sip of the soup had gotten him choked and suffocated in his windpipe. Sarah had immediately handed him a glass of water; her facial expression, kind words, love, and care had obliviated his intention. Having not met such gracious people in his life, the sudden caress of motherliness had confused him. He looked at her and said, "Thank you." "My mom is so sweet; she'll take care of everybody as how she'd take care of her child. Don't worry; you'll get to know more about her," said Sandra gently. Deep down, Shawn is a wolf in sheep's clothing, ready to tear down and devour his prey. Even though that was his real nature, Sarah's kindness and biblical conditioning of showing love even to her enemies and her concern with hospitality pacified him temporarily. He was speechless, stood up, and said, "Well, I gotta go now. Thanks for lunch!" He came out of the door. As he opened the main gate, Sandra dragged him by his hand and hugged him tightly. The front window of the red Toyota right across the house was sliding down; Martin was sitting in the car and watching everything.

Shawn got into the car; no one had spoken a word to him. Upon arriving at their motel, Martin had descended from the car before everyone could and slammed the door behind him. He literally pulled Shawn through the window and threw him out. He browbeat him harshly, drew the gun from his back, and almost blew his head. Shawn begged him for life, "Stop it, stop it! Please let me explain. I didn't do anything intentionally."

"I have taken a lot of effort to get the diamonds, which you can never imagine. Do you remember why we are here and what we promised Ricardo? The next time you kill them and get the diamonds if anything goes wrong. I'll never be reluctant to pull the trigger," said Martin exasperatedly.

Sarah phoned Debbie and told her about Shawn; she was very much interested in meeting him and asked her to invite him to her house for lunch. Sandra phoned him immediately.

"My mom likes you a lot. She usually doesn't trust anybody, and you're the first person she wants to meet again. You're not a stranger anymore; you're a part of our family. Actually, my mom told her best friend about us, and she invited you for lunch at her house tomorrow. She's a very sweet person. You must meet her." Said Sandra

"Sorry, sweetheart, I wish I could, but I have to go to New York for a business trip, so I thought of meeting you and your mom before I leave," said Shawn empathetically. Sandra agreed with him too.

There was no change of plan. All three of them had headed to Sarah's Ville and parked the car at the same spot. Shawn got down and looked at the house, but this time he was well-prepared, and the demon inside himself was wide awake. As it was a bright sunny day in the morning, they had set the table outside the house for coffee with cookies. But Shawn refused the idea and called them inside to have a little chat before he could leave. Sarah led him to the house while Sandra carried the tray with kettles, cups, and cookies. She kept the tray on the table and asked him to have a seat with a wide smile. He smashed the tray off the table and threw the chairs away, and asked, "Where are the diamonds?" Sarah felt those words as claps of thunderstorms echoed across the room. The fear that she was dreading had come to reality. Shawn had shown his true colors and unleashed the vampire, which had been hiding for the right moment. Sarah and Sandra were struck with fear and looked at him in consternation. He asked them about the diamonds again. "We don't have any diamonds. You'd come to the wrong place. Leave us alone. I'm going to call the police right now," said Sarah. Before she could use her cell phone to dial 911, he drew the gun out and shot twice at the ceiling, which made her drop the phone on the floor and stand still. The gunfire had signaled Martin and Ron to jump into the picture.

* * *

Sandra continues...

My mother was dismayed to see Martin. "You're a betrayer! You're a murderer. You killed my husband," she cried. "If you tell us where the diamonds are, no one would get hurt. Otherwise, you'd see a river of blood in your house before you die," said Martin evilly. Shawn held my hair and dragged me while Ron put the gun into my mouth and said, "I will count to three, and I want you to say where the diamonds are. Otherwise, I'll blow your head in front of your mother." My mother was terrified to see me with a gun stuck in my mouth. She took the kettle and threw the hot coffee onto Ron's face. He dropped the gun and covered his face with his two hands, and screamed in pain. Martin was aggravated and held my mother by her throat, took her off the ground, and thrust her forcefully against the wall. She banged her head hard and slid down to the floor. Streaks of blood flowed from the back of her head and matted onto the floor. Her eyes were stunned, without any reaction. "If you don't give the diamonds, your daughter will be raped in front of your eyes." There was no response from my mother, and I was scared to death.

* * *

Sandra pauses for a moment. Her eyes turn red, and tears roll down uncontrollably. Maria tries to comfort her, gives her tissue paper, and hands her a glass of water. "If you're not comfortable, that's fine, my dear. You may take some rest now," says Pastor Williams. "No, Father, that's fine! I'm alright," says Sandra and continues.

* * *

I wasn't bound or gagged but controlled at gunpoint by Ron. My mom was breathless, leaning against the wall without a blink of her eyes. I begged them to save my mom, but they didn't care and didn't even allow me to touch her. I also told them the truth that the diamonds were not there with us and promised that I'd take them to where it is. "Do I look like an idiot? Don't try to trick me like your dad. I know the diamonds are here with you," said Martin. I told them the truth many times, but they didn't believe me at all. The house was ransacked. They broke the closet, drawer, and wardrobe. They tore the pillows and matrasses but found nothing. They crushed everything in the house and got nothing left; all of them became furious. As the diamonds were not found anywhere in the house, their attention turned toward me. Ron went to my mom and pushed her cheek with his foot. She fell down like a wet log. They laughed at each other. Ron slapped me many times, tore my clothes off, and got me naked. Shawn was holding my hands while Martin raped me brutally. They took turns and molested me without any mercy. Ron had scavenged cigarette butts on my body, but my mom's silence was more painful than the cigarette burns. It was like three hyenas feasting up on a live gazelle. I was bleeding through my private part but nothing stopped them from crushing me.

A car honked on the spur of the moment, and the doorbell rang. They got terrified; Martin asked me who that was, which I had no idea about. I had no strength to speak a word and didn't know who was standing behind the door, but I decided to turn the situation in my favor. So I said, "Police officers! They check in every day at this time to ensure we are safe." Immediately, they looked at each other panicky, signaled with their eyes, and scooted through the back door. With immense pain, I gathered myself up from the floor with the dripping blood from all over my body and crawled to reach my mom. I had no courage to see her face. Her eyes were still and remained open. Her silence was tearing my ears. I immediately checked her pulse and heartbeat, but it was nothing, and she was very cold. I wanted to resuscitate her, but it was too late. The doorbell was still ringing. I teetered to the door and looked through the peephole. Debbie and Simon were standing outside. Things in the house were shattered, and a pool of blood was all over the floor. I got back to my mom and laid down next to her without being able to move my body an inch.

I knew Simon desperately wanted to see me; he would have given Debbie a hard time taking him to my house.

That's why she had brought him home, but I couldn't help it because it would be a trauma for an autistic kid to witness such an incident. After hours of crying, I decided to take a step forward and, at the same time, didn't want to extinguish the conflagration that was burning inside me. We tried protecting the diamonds not because it was worth a fortune but because it was a souvenir from my dad, as he gave them in his last breath. If he had given me six pebbles from the seashore, I would treat them the same way I treat these diamonds. If I had those gems in my hand, I would have thrown them in their face because my mom's life is more important to me than the diamonds. I told them the truth countless times, but they didn't trust me. Even if I'd given them the diamonds, they would've done the same thing.

They had already caused enough physical and mental damage and killed three of my important family members, the lives that are very important to me. I had never thought of going to the police because it didn't make sense to me. Whenever the police get involved, the media will be involved too and blow things beyond proportion; they would dig everything up, the past life of my father and grandfather, and accuse us of possessing these precious diamonds. Moreover, I can at least fulfill my dad's wish and keep the diamonds safe. The love I have for my dad is unconditional, even when he was vituperative, because the good days I spent with him are still fresh in my heart.

Chapter 6

At Bowersville

"Why am I supposed to go through all this? Why don't I deserve to live a normal life just like everyone else?" Although these questions often pop up in Sandra's mind, she clearly knows that it's wise to accept reality rather than dwell on the past, so she made up her mind to focus on the solution and go forward in life. Rolled up her mother in a blanket and put her in the back seat of her car. If there was a better place on the earth for Sarah, it would be Bowersville, where her husband Daniel had rested in peace. She was on her way with her mother's corpse, driving fast with immense pain in her body, mind, and soul. Those trees, roads, and the narrow bridge reminded her of the last time she went there with her mother. Now, she was at the place where nobody lived except some birds and animals. Her hands trembled as she was in anguish; it was extremely difficult for her to dig the gravel pit even though the soil was loose and wet. Finally, she did the exact same thing that her mother had done for Daniel. Sarah had read the bible for Daniel's peace while Sandra stood bowing her head down for prayers. Now, she was doing everything by her own bootstraps.

Sandra was exhausted and sat on the ground next to her parents' garden of burial. She pensively looked at the key in her hand and the door of the house. She decided to spend the night there. It was so lonesome. The lights were flickered. The bats were shattered, and spider webs were all over the ceilings and walls. She used to go there with her mother once a year on her father's Remembrance Day. Now, she's stranded all alone to fend for herself. Betrayed and brutally raped, her only guardian angel, her mom, was ruthlessly killed, and the thought of being an orphan brought inconsolable sorrows and tears to Sandra.

Sandra is optimistic and always looks at the brighter side of every situation. She's not a pond but a river that flows constantly. She has a spirit with the quality of water. No matter how hard it gets banged by anything, it'll never collapse but regain its shape, keep going, and flourish everywhere it sets its presence.

Her thoughts presided as to what had to be done. She had never checked the diamonds ever since her mother had hidden them in a secret locker. The rooms in the house were not like those in typical American dwellings. It was specially designed to store valuable gems and important documents. Her mother had always forbidden her to explore the entire house. It seems to be a complex maze to her, even with a complete plan of the house. Antonio gave the map of the adobe to Daniel; he handed it to Sarah, and now Sandra got the map in her hand and was looking at it scrupulously. The narrow passage led to a stairwell to the basement. The sound of her footsteps increased her heartbeat as it echoed. She had never been afraid when she went with her mom because she always felt protected and confident under her mother's wings.

At last, she reached the locker and carefully opened it. There she was, with the most precious, valuable, and glittering diamonds in her hands. Three important people that she cherished the most had lost their lives for it. Her father's voice was still echoing in her ears. "Never lose these diamonds. These are ours. Your grandfather lost his life for it. Keep them safe and leave this place forever." Even Sarah would've revealed where the diamonds were if Martin hadn't pushed her against the wall. She would never take any chances with her daughter's life, and Martin was aware of her integrity and would've believed her without hesitation.

It was heartbreaking for Sandra to think of her mother's horrifying death, but she was trying to synchronize her aching body and worn-out soul. In the perception of failure, the fight always lies between the heart and mind. While her heart drools in self-pity that Shawn had betrayed her, her mind demands justice. In times of hardship, reconciliation with oneself is hard as harmony has lost its natural realm; thus, unable to avoid the raging war between the heart and mind.

The night seemed long and gloomy as Sandra had never spent even a few hours there without her mother. The blazing inferno in herself didn't spare her to be in peace but to take revenge and burn everyone down to ashes, which she had no idea how to do. She was restless and wandering inside the house the whole night, but it had already dawned before she could get any clues.

As a wounded soul with no family or friends to turn to, the only shoulder to cry on was her mom's friend Debbie; but she couldn't reach out to her even though she badly wanted to because she looked like a stamped-on rose that could raise many questions. Moreover, she didn't want Debbie's family to get involved in it. Thus, she had to avoid her. She spent a long night in Bowersville and headed back to her house, especially to clean up the mess. There was nobody waiting for her back home. She couldn't find any difference between the graveyard in Bowersville and her house in Rockville. It looked the same to her, depressing and silent. The blood stains were all over the floor. Almost all the items were broken, and her mother's cry was echoing in her ears like the stings of a thousand wasps. Mopped the floor three times, packed all the smashed-up items, and dumped them in the basement storeroom.

The house was almost empty but clean. She was hungry and tired and hadn't eaten anything since the incident. There were some bread and butter left in the kitchen room. She got a glimpse of her cell phone while making a toast. Many missed calls and messages from Martin. One of them was a video message about her getting raped. Their faces were blurred but not hers. Another message from him stated: "We want to meet you at 7 pm at Square Park. If you don't show up, your video will be circulated across your college and on the internet. If you try anything stupid, the repercussions will be more severe than you can ever imagine." Sandra was exasperated and shocked to see the video, the bloodstains, the scream, and her wounded mother; everything was edited, and they created it as if she did that with her own consent. "I want to kill them…I want to kill them. I want to kill them," her voice trembled with outrage. Before she could agree, she looked up the meeting spot on the internet that Martin proposed. It's an open bar where people would be around. "Okay, will meet you there," replied Sandra

Sandra arrived at the spot a little earlier, wearing a brown fringe jacket, ripped jeans, sunglasses, zipper calf-high winter boots, and a hat. She sat on a chair with her legs crossed. Although there were bruises all over her body, one of her eyes was marked blue. Blood shots on her pale wrists and the rawness of the cigarette butts revealed that she had been under trauma lately, but she appeared more confident than ever before and was determined to get things even. The three men arrived, looking for her. She was calm and composed, just looking at them standing before her. She snapped her fingers to grab their attention. One of them turned back. She leaned back on the chair and rested her left elbow on its arm, and gestured for them to come to the table. She removed the hat, wiggled her hair a bit, pointed her hand at the chairs in front of her, and gesticulated for them to sit. They took their seats. Ron opened one side of his jacket and showed her the gun.

She gave him a sardonic smile and said, "I'm not scared of anything now. I lost everybody, and I got nothing to lose. You wanna blow my head? Be my guest! Do it right now, but guess what? Those diamonds will be lost forever. If you do what I say, you can get what you want, and I will find my way out of this." Martin pressed Ron's thigh, signaled him to be quiet, and asked her, "Alright, tell us what you got to say. If you have any intentions to deceive us, your video will be published, and we won't let you live your life." She said, "I don't have them here in Rockville." Ron got angry and took the gun out. Sandra fumed; her eyes behind the glasses turned red. She stood up, banged her hand on the table, and screamed, "Shoot me! Come on, shoot me. I'm standing in front of you. Come on, go ahead." People around them started paying attention. Martin clinched Ron's wrist to be quiet and asked her to sit down. "Look, if I had an intention of going to the police, I wouldn't have come here alone. Do you think I would get a better chance than this to get you all apprehended? That's not my intention. This is the fact whether you believe me or not." She told them to come to her house on Sunday, and Martin didn't want to wrangle but agreed with her.

Sandra didn't expect Martin would agree with her, he had to because she didn't give him a choice. Martin wanted to handle it in his way as he had the confidence that she can't get away from him. Now she had to plan everything for perfect execution. She read many books, watched many movies, and ruminated for a long time, but nothing worked out. She went to bed despondently, but the dream she had in her sleep had brought her a new aspiration. It was a perfect blueprint. The following day, she visualized the whole thing and realized it was the ideal stratagem. She searched the internet for the best pet shop and found one, but it was too far. She phoned the shop owner and confirmed if she could get the most ferocious dog breed in the States. The shop owner had assured her they have all types of dogs, from the tamest to the most dangerous breed. Sandra went to the shop by a rented minivan to be able to take four grown dogs: an American pit bull, two Rottweilers, and a Presa Canarios. "They can get very aggressive and even kill anybody who stands in their way, so beware of them," said the shop owner. She was so happy to hear him saying 'can kill anybody,' and took them in her van to Bowersville. All the flowers on the burial ground were still fresh; she stood in front of the crosses where her parents were buried. With her tear-filled eyes, she took the warriors into the house. She also got the required tools to alter the room, such as ripping bars, oscillating multi-tool, sledgehammers, short iron doors, five long iron chains, pipes, tanks, powerful hand drillers, sprinklers, and sensors. All the rooms in the house were sound and lightproof; it took more than fifteen hours for her to set the trap. The dogs were fed and also got a sack full of bones, water, and dry food to keep them healthy. Sandra clearly knew that these types of dogs don't have to be hungry to attack anybody. It was all set; she checked them multiple times to make sure that they worked perfectly; they were as accurate as she expected. A CCTV camera was installed in the dog's room to have an eye on them, and she also brought a network booster to connect the camera to her cell phone directly, as that area had a weak signal.

Sandra got a voicemail from Debbie in a panic-stricken voice, "Simon's met with an accident, and we are at the Seven Hills hospital. He's in the ICU. I called Sarah, but her number was not reachable. I wish you were here with us. He would feel better if he saw you." She locked the house and immediately went to the hospital at breakneck speed. Debbie and Cathy were sitting in the emergency ward.

"What happened? How is he now?" asked Sandra quaveringly.

"I just stopped by the supermarket to get some groceries. He suddenly opened the door, got out, and was hit by a car woefully. He's got AB negative, which is a rare blood group. Unfortunately, the hospital is out of stock now. They asked me to find a donor. I contacted everyone I know, but no one is AB negative," said Debbie in a brittle manner.

Sandra held Debbie's hands and said, "Did you say AB negative? I'm AB negative too; I can be his donor." She thanked God and hugged her warmly for the timely help.

Debbie noticed something was wrong and asked her what had happened and where Sarah was. But Sandra didn't answer any of Debbie's questions. "Everything is fine; don't worry about us. Let's focus on Simon now. We need to save him," said Sandra and headed to donate blood.

A blood transfusion was done. Debbie, Sandra, and Cathy were sitting outside the ER lobby, praying for Simon's speedy recovery. As a thunderbolt, Sandra saw all three of them, Martin, Ron, and Shawn, at the Nurses Station. She panicked to see them just a few meters away and thought they were following her, so she left the place in the state of bewilderment and hastened into the changing room; she peeped through the window to see if the coast was clear, and yes, it certainly was. Her phone was ringing, and she took the call. "Honey, where are you? You were not there when I opened my eyes from prayer. What's happening? Is everything alright, sweetheart?" "Yes, yes, nothing to worry about. I gotta go now. Please do me a favor. If anybody asks anything about me, just tell them that you don't know anyone called Sandra. And please message me if there's anything important." "You saved my son's life; I will never forget it. Don't worry, sweetheart. God is with you. You, please carry on." Martin, as well as his buddies, had only come there to visit their friend, and it was mere coincidence that she had spotted them.

After arriving home, she called Debbie to check if anyone had asked for her at the hospital, but none. Sandra was very concerned about the safety of Debbie's family, and she didn't want the trio to know she was Debbie's family friend. She returned to Bowersville with five kilograms of pepper powder, three gallons of petrol, and ten giant rolls of aluminum foil to insulate the walls and ceiling. She also bought a speaker to install in the room.

With a tired body, aching feet, and weary soul, the rage in her heart had fueled her to continue working without rest. It'd been several days since she had slept well, and her heart was permeated with revenge. The only thing that echoes in her mind was: "I will never rest until I bring them to ashes." Messages were pouring into her inbox, and a new message popped up. Sandra got irritated and opened the WhatsApp: "Where are you?" She did not reply. He sent her another message: "I'm repeating you. Don't ever think of doing anything stupid! You know me very well." "I think I made my point clear in our last meeting. You will get the diamonds, and you need to trust me on this. All I want is to get out of this once and for all. Let me tell you something. I don't want to receive any more messages from you. Come tomorrow at 6 p.m. I will take you to where the diamonds are."

At 6 pm, Sandra took all three of them to Bowersville. She was well-prepared, ready with night vision glasses and remote control in her pocket. The door to hell had opened; she went in first, followed by the other three men. After a moment, all the lights were off, and the room was filled with darkness. There was no way that they could see each other.

They panicked and were ready to pull the trigger. She wore her night vision glasses and took the iron rod, which was readily kept in the corner of the room. She held the rod and smashed their hands. She quickly got out of the room with their guns and closed the automatic doors.

The speaker was on. Sandra spoke, "Hey, Martin, Shawn, and Ron! Please don't panic. I'm going to introduce you to four of my new friends. Just be nice to them." The small iron doors were opened from each corner of the room; it was placed in such a way that the dog's chain wouldn't get entangled with each other. All four murderous predators were set out in the dark room, waiting to taste the blood. A small incandescent red light bulb was switched on that blinked constantly. The whole room was filled with the color of the blood, which agitated the dogs deftly. They attacked all three of them dreadfully, ripped their skins, and bit them all over their body. She didn't want them to be killed only by the dogs. So, the dogs were pulled back to their cages and closed the door by the remote control. Now she turned on the sprinklers, which sprinkled the hot pepper oil in the entire room. They were mindlessly leaping and crying in pain. They continuously banged on the door for help. Nothing was visible inside the room except the darkness. The loud wailing ceased when the speaker was turned on. Sandra spoke, "This is how I felt when you all raped me. I had pain, and you all had the pleasure. Now, you all are in pain, and I'm having the pleasure of watching you suffer." Pepper oil sprinklers were turned off. And then the new sprinklers connected to the petrol tank were turned on. "I'm going to turn on the fuel nozzle. Have fun." The fuel nozzles were turned on, and they sprayed petrol throughout the room. Martin, Shawn, and Ron got drenched in the fuel. The ceiling and walls were perfectly sealed with high fire-resistant aluminum foil. They were swamped in blood, pepper oil, and petrol.

Finally, she switched on the ignition spark plug, which was fixed in the corner of the ceiling. The entire room was set on fire, and all three of them, Martin, Shawn, and Ron, were burned down to ashes.

Sandra was startled by the nightmare and woke up sweating profusely. Sitting on the bed and looking at her own room with anxiety, she couldn't recognize where she was, gasping for breath and looking at the clock; it was a quarter past two. It took her a few moments to realize it was a horrific dream. Everything she saw, spoke, and did felt like it had happened for real, but it was just a dream.

Sharply at 6 pm, a loud honk was heard in front of Sarah's Ville, but there was no sign of anybody coming out of the house. Martin got agitated, pressed the horn twice, and took a cell phone to call her. There was another car ahead of them. A hand popped out of the window and gave a signal to follow.

All three of them got their guns ready; Martin forbore his anger and asked Ron to follow her car. They were amazed by her driving skill on the highway; the destination arrived after a long drive. Martin asked Shawn and Ron to check if there was anyone else in that place, but no one was there other than the four of them. They got their guns out; Shawn pointed the gun at her to go ahead. She opened the wooden gate with the keys and looked at them unflinchingly. Everyone followed her into the house. It looked so mysterious;

their level of suspicion had increased as she took them to the basement.

She vividly remembered everything she'd done in her dreams and was well-prepared to do it exactly the same way. She got the night glasses and the remote control ready in her pocket. The door to hell had opened. She went in first, followed by the three of them. Suddenly, the lights were off, and the room was filled with darkness. They were panicking as they couldn't see anything. "Hey, where are you? What are you doing? Switch on the lights. We can't see anything." All three of them cried in fear. They took the pistols and tried to pull the trigger in dread; she could see things as she was wearing night vision glasses. Sandra grabbed the iron rod, which was kept in the corner of the room, smashed their hands, got out of the room with their guns, and closed the automatic door.

Sitting outside the room on a wooden chair with the remote control of the small iron gates of killer dogs, pepper oil sprinklers, fuel sprinklers, and spark plugs. Although she was determined to execute the plan, her conscience pricked her. She was sweating blood and got cold feet as the teachings of the bible, and her mother's words didn't permit her to take revenge. Unable to do what she had intended, she was crying, holding her head down in shame as she heard her mother's voice, and all that she'd taught her was echoing in her ears.

The dogs were constantly barking and hitting the grilled gate. The three men were scared and anxious; they didn't know what was going to happen next. The room was pitch dark and completely sealed that they couldn't escape. Submerged in long thoughts, opened her eyes and turned on the speaker that was connected inside the room. Her inconsolable sobs filled the room. The dogs became silent. The loudspeakers amplify her weeps in the concealed room. The trio was shivering and had no clue what was going on. The cry faded. "With just a click of a button, I can release all the dogs. You will be bitten mercilessly, and your bones will be crushed by their powerful jaws. Another click of a button will open the pepper oil and the fuel tank that would burn you all down to ashes, but I'm not gonna do that because I'm a God's child. I was loved by my dad, I was loved by my mom, and I was taught to love others regardless of their flaws. I'm not a monster or predator like you all. I don't wanna make the same mistake you all have made. Otherwise, there won't be any difference between you and me. I forgive you all. I got the gun in my hand, and I'm gonna open the door now; just run away and get out of my life," said Sandra.

She opened the door without counting on the costly repercussions of setting them free; they mindlessly staggered out of the room by pushing each other to save their own lives. She held the gun straight and escorted them to the exit. It was a dark and stormy night. There was no sign of any pathway. The land was wet and slippery as it was raining. In spite of that, they plodded fast into the woods. The rain picked up; lightning flashed and pushed its inverted limb down to the woods. Within a few seconds, a loud boom of thunder struck the place. The trees were wobbling by a strong wind, and the wheezing sound haunted the area. Their hands were injured and bleeding because Sandra had hit them with an iron rod to fling the guns away. Martin took the lead downhill, followed by Shawn and Ron. Accidentally, Ron slipped and pushed the others; all three of them fell and went tumbling down the slope and ended up in a bottomless pit of quicksand. Everyone cried, "Help! Help! Help!"

* * *

Sandra continues…

I heard a dreadful voice of help; I immediately went there, despite the downpour, as the surroundings were pretty familiar to me. I was shocked to see them stuck in the quicksand, almost sucked up to their neck. But by the time I rushed to them, they were completely swallowed by it. I trudged to my parents' gravestone and hunkered down there, wailing out my pain in the rain.

Pastor Williams was stunned, and Maria stood up and applauded her.

I cleared up everything and moved back to Rockville to start a new life. I spent most of my time in Debbie's house with Simon and Cathy. One day, when I was playing on the seesaw with the kids in a nearby park, I suddenly fainted on the ground. The children panicked, and luckily there was another guy playing with his kids, too; he rushed me to the nearby hospital.

I was shocked to hear the news from the doctor. I'd been pregnant for three months. The doctor handed over my result, but I couldn't even hold it, and it slipped from my hands as I was in great shock. I was young, too young to have a kid. I dreaded thinking of raising a baby on my own. The doctor smelled something wrong; she thought I would go for an abortion, but I didn't do that. I wanted to take responsibility and raise my baby by myself.

Debbie used to come once in a while to check how I was coping. One day, she asked me about my mom and how I ended up getting pregnant. I was not ready to tell her anything about what had happened. I told her, "I can't say anything right now, but I would definitely share everything with you when I want to. So, please don't ask me anything." From then on, she never asked me anything, which was one of the reasons I liked her the most.

After the tragedy, I spent most of my time with Simon and Cathy in Debbie's house to forget the horrendous incident as well as to get away from the depression. Sarah's Ville seemed to be a pain and sorrow in my eyes. Every corner of the house reminded me of my time with my mom. Her screams reverberated all the time in my mind when I was in that house. After I came to know that I had another life inside me, I decided to relocate and destroy all of my past contacts. I couldn't continue my studies as I was pregnant and broke. I also didn't want to get help from Debbie or use my dad's and mom's influence to find work. With great persistence, I was able to find a job at Stan's Inc. in Baltimore. Far and behold, I relocated there, leaving everything behind both in thought and deed. The ambiance, work, and co-staff kept me on my toes; it also helped me to procure new things and to move on in life.

As my due date was nearing, I found a lot of changes in my body. I couldn't walk as I used to. I couldn't eat or breathe as I used to. The feeling of overwrought and fatigue was ineluctable. I was dreadful and anxious as I had never had such an experience, but I managed to do things independently.

Nine missed calls and many messages and voicemails on my cell phone. All were from Debbie.

I called her back, and she said, "Hey, sweetheart! How are you? The due date is approaching. I'm worried about you, honey. Please come to Rockville for your confinement. I know there won't be anybody to look after you. Please, don't say no. Love you."

I had never dreamed of going back to Rockville, but I had to say 'yes' to Debbie as I didn't want to offend her and also for the safe delivery of my daughter. I strictly told her not to tell Simon about my arrival because I didn't want to break his heart again. It was not easy for me either. Also, I requested her not to visit me often. I stayed in Sara's Ville all the time except for the doctor's visit. Debbie planned to send her children to her aunt's house to be with me at the time of the parturition, but that didn't happen. It was about 10 p.m.; I had cramps and increased back pain, urinated constantly, walked across the house, and was in fear of delivery complications. I searched for my cell phone to call Debbie. But my water broke, and I was in severe pain, with the contractions becoming stronger since they started to occur every two minutes. With the significant pressure in the abdomen and pelvic region, I knew the baby was descending. My energy levels were deteriorating, and I was unable to rest or relax between my contractions. The intensity of the sharp pain rose together with the stinging sensation in my uterus. I felt a strong urge to push with my last intake of breath, and behold. My princess wailed out her first cry before Debbie arrived.

Chapter 7

At York Shrine

The room is quiet. Father Williams and Maria can't find a better word to console Sandra, and she doesn't expect that either. She feels much better now as if she had gotten rid of tons of loads she had been carrying for many years. "Thank you so much for patiently listening to me, Father. Maria, you're such a kind woman," says Sandra. "I have served the Lord and been a 'Father' in many congregations for more than a couple of decades. I've listened to many stories of people from all walks of life: relentless murderers, ruthless molesters, and remorseless deceivers. I still receive an account of their sins and undertake to give them absolution, but you, my child, have deliberately chosen to forgive them regardless of the serious offense they did against you. This will empower you to be able to lose your corrosive anger to walk as per our doctrine. May the Lord bless you and your daughter! May His guarding Angels guard and guide you all! "In the same way, Let your light so shine before others so that people may see your good work and glorify your Father in heaven! I ask all this in the name of the Father, the Son, and the Holy Spirit; Amen," says Father.

Sandra is now pondering the fact that she has to deal with another one now; she knows that the guy who's in search of her must be Ricardo.

She says to herself, "I'm ready to meet you at any time, Ricardo. I'll do anything to give my daughter a safer life."

"I feel so sorry for what you have gone through. You are the most courageous woman I've ever met in my life. I'm really proud of you. Actually, I was talking to Father Williams. It looks like he's more concerned about the safety of the people in our church, and he's indeed worried about you as well. He told me to ask you if you could hand over those diamonds to the cops, then all the problems would be solved. The person who's hunting for you won't have any reason to find you. Please don't ever think we will disseminate whatever you told us. Everything will be absolutely confidential," says Maria. "I'm glad you brought that to me, and I will surely think about it," Sandra replies.

They live in a very small room which can just occupy a single cot and a small crib for Merlin, and there's hardly a place for her daughter to play around, but she's always been grateful for what she has, and that is what shaped her as who she's now. Sandra begins to think like a mom who always prioritizes her child's safety and security. Being a single mom is an added responsibility to take care of her daughter. So, she wants to use a different strategy to handle this situation.

She remembers the paper that father Williams handed her. It has Ricardo's phone number. She calls the number but reaches voicemail, "Hey Ricardo, it's me. The one you are looking for; call me back." He calls her right after he checks the message, but Sandra purposely diverts his call to the voicemail to read what is on his mind. "I'm surprised you've recognized me without seeing my face. I know you're a clever woman. I have no intention of hurting you or your child. Return my call at the earliest," says Ricardo. Sandra learns about him from her father but hasn't seen him in person. Now that she has gotten Merlin with her, she has to take every step more cautiously. Everyone in her family was murdered mercilessly, and now she's only got her daughter, a person whom she can call a family.

Afraid of losing any more precious lives, she intends to meet him at a common place where many people would gather often. Ricardo is in his early seventies with gray hair but looks athletic. She sits opposite him and appears valiantly. "I'm glad you came. I'm just gonna ask you two questions, and I expect a genuine answer from you." "Please, go ahead," replies Sandra. "Where are the diamonds? Where are my three men?" asks Ricardo gravely. Sandra stands up on her feet and looks astonished. "What are you talking about? You sent your men to take the diamonds, and they killed my mom, molested me mercilessly, and took all the six diamonds that I got from my father. I lost my dad; my mom and I were raped by them inhumanly. As a result, I'm raising a child who doesn't know who her father is, and neither do I. They are not kids to be lost forever. I heard Martin saying many times, 'Those are my diamonds.' I think they betrayed you." Ricardo takes his hat, flings it on the table, and screams, "I knew it. I knew it. I had a doubt when he avoided me accompanying them when they left for Rockville. Do you know where they possibly are? Did they say anything about that?" asks Ricardo. "Honestly, I have no idea where they are. I'm lucky that they spared my life. After I surrendered the diamonds to Martin, I thought everything was over and didn't expect that you'd come for it. If you still don't trust me, you're searching for it in the wrong place," says Sandra.

Ricardo believed everything that Sandra told him because she matched things perfectly and gave no room for him to suspect her. After he leaves the place, she breathes a sigh of relief and starts to break down. Curtailing her loud sobs from within to avoid getting noticed by the people around her, she hurries off with a mixture of emotions and anxiety about what will happen next. With the hope that he will be able to get the diamonds back from the trio, Ricardo pursues his search. She hasn't told anybody that she would meet the man hunting for her with a gun, so no one is expecting her at the church other than Merlin. Merlin tiptoes her soft foot onto her mother and hugs her firmly; Sandra is overwhelmed with happiness to see her child walking.

Life has been a run around in circles for Sandra. She has been relocating from one place to another since childhood but never broods over it. Even though it's just less than a year, Sandra and her daughter Merlin have many good memories at the York Shrine Church, and they met many wonderful people there who showed true love and care. However, the horrific incident of searching for her child in the park and the fear of losing her daughter has made Sandra find a new place for shelter. In order to protect the child from the smuggler and provide her with a sophisticated life, she has made the decision to leave the church. She always wanted to move to an individual house or an apartment where her child would find it more comfortable and lives like every other little one. The York Shrine church had been a gift for Sandra. She never underestimated it and will truly remember the church and the people, especially father Williams and Maria, as long as she's alive.

Chapter 8

A Sunrise in Texas

More than half a decade has passed since they moved to Houston, Texas. It is one of the most beautiful cities in the south-central part of the USA. Sandra works in a private school as a kindergarten teacher in the city where her daughter also studies. Life has never been easier for single parents, especially the ones who have no support from their parents, relatives, or even friends. She has been facing all the good and bad days just by herself. She hasn't made any friends ever since she moved to Texas, not even in touch with Maria back in York Shrine, nor with Debbie in Rockville. She always stays on the fringe of all relationships except with her daughter. None of her colleagues was invited to her house, be it on Thanksgiving, Christmas, or even New Year. Even though she is more concerned about safety, like her mother, Sarah, she couldn't completely isolate her daughter from her friends. Merlin wants to celebrate her birthday with all of her friends and doesn't give an opportunity to Sandra to deny that; Sandra knows how it feels to be away from everything because she had been through the same situation in her childhood. So, she threw a party at home and invited only a few close friends of Merlin, who are very familiar with Sandra too. Although life has been cruel to Sandra, she finds happiness in her daughter's eyes. Every little thing about Merlin brings immense joy to her more than anything else in the world. She always relishes seeing every step her daughter takes to go to the next level in her life.

The best thing about having her daughter studying in the same place where she works is that she doesn't have to look out for anyone to take care of her during the school holidays. She takes her to school and leaves her in the library or playground, where she can play games or read some comics. Merlin is one of the most active and fun-loving kids in the classroom and has a tit-for-tat attitude, like her grandfather. While doing an activity that involves teamwork, she unexpectedly bites her peer on his thigh. She nibbles him so hard that it makes him cry out loud, which can even be heard by his father, who works at the restaurant. The bitten area becomes red, and so does his face; the tiny teeth impression on his pale skin makes it more obvious to anyone who could easily figure it out.

"I told you many times not to play with the pet animals. See, now, you got bitten by a puppy," says George.

"No, dad, I wasn't bitten by any puppies but by a stupid little girl called Merlin. She thinks she's the most beautiful and clever girl in the school, but she's not dad, she's not. I hate her daddy; I don't know, for some reason, I get so scared to talk to her sometimes," says Billy.

George's telling his son that he will go to school with him, talk to Merlin, warn her mother to discipline her child, and get it straightened up.

The next day, George takes Billy to the school to talk to the principal and the class teacher. As they enter the school premises, Billy ducks down and says in a low voice, "There she is! Dad, that's Merlin in the blue car. Pull over, pull over! Let them go in first." "Don't be scared, Billy. I'll take care of it." As he reaches the school early before the bell rings, George meets Sandra in the office room and asks, "I need to see the principal right now. Could you tell me where he is?" "The principal doesn't meet the parents without an appointment and he's not available now and won't be for the next three days." As George is with Billy, Sandra asks him if he's Billy's father. "Yes, I am," says George. "I'm his class teacher. You may tell me what's in regards to," says Sandra. "My son didn't sleep the whole night; he was getting nightmare after nightmare. He was terribly bitten by a kid called Merlin in your class," says George. "I'm aware of it, and the girl that you're talking about is my daughter."

"Oh, is it, so you failed both as a teacher and as a mother to teach your kid manners?" Merlin stands next to Sandra, which grabs George's attention. "All right, is she the one who'd bitten my son?" Merlin starts crying in fear and says, "No, he was the one who started first; he broke my paper can and made fun of it." "I see! My son is capable of doing that stuff. Now I understand who the culprit is," says George, but she doesn't stop crying. George tries to calm her down and says, "Honey, listen. Why are you crying now? That's all right. It happens, sweetheart. I can totally understand that. He shouldn't have broken your paper can in the first place, and you shouldn't have bitten him too. Anyway, we all make mistakes, but let's not repeat them. I'll talk to my son, and guess what? He will be good to you. You can trust me on that." She doesn't seem to be convinced but is weeping very badly. Sandra stands next to her daughter with folded hands and looks at him angrily. "All right, I'm gonna tell you a real story that happened in my life. Have you ever experienced real pain, I mean the pain of getting bitten by a dog? I have. On a random Friday, I was on a couch, watching Star Wars and having a giant pizza with molten cheese and too much mayonnaise. In spite of watching an interesting movie, I fell asleep with mayonnaise and cheese all over my mouth. I had two dogs, Ruuney and Tuuney. Unfortunately, both of them were unchained. First, Runney came over and started licking my mouth, then the greedy Tuuney pushed Runney away and wanted to lick the big portion of mayonnaise, but apparently, it got away with my mouth," says George dramatically. Both Sandra and Merlin burst out into laughter. Sandra couldn't control herself, and he continued, "I know about my son and the kids these days, but as a teacher, it's your duty to have an eye on them to make sure they don't hurt each other." "First of all, let me apologize for what my daughter did to your son. Secondly, you better learn to take care of yourself by not letting any dogs lick or bite your mouth before advising someone else. Now, I guarantee you that your son will not have any problems with my daughter," says Sandra.

Later, in the classroom, she calls both the kids and tells them to be friendly with one another. "Good kids will always share love and joy, but the bad apples are the ones who fight with each other. Which ones would you guys like to be, good apples or bad apples?" They both shout, "Good apple, good apple!" The words "you failed as a teacher and as a mother" stuck in her head. "How can someone be so mean to someone who they barely know or just met for the first time? I just hate that guy, and I don't want to see him again." But Sandra doesn't discriminate against his son; she treats all the kids equally and takes good care of them. Merlin and Billy become good friends; they spend more time together playing at the school's playground after class hours because she has to wait for her mother for about an hour to finish her work, and so does Billy. His father works at a restaurant, and he is also a part-time real estate agent. So, he usually comes late to pick him up. Billy would get angry with his father whenever he arrived late in the evening to receive him from school, but nowadays, he doesn't care as he enjoys spending time with Merlin. "How come you aren't mad at me? I'm very, very late than usual," asks George. "It's alright, dad. You're cool. You can come whenever you want. Take your own time, daddy. I have a good companion at school, and I have a nice time with her," says Billy enthusiastically. "Oh yeah, is it? Look at you; when did that happen? Alright, who is she? You never told me anything about her," says George. "Come on, dad. You know her. She was the one who bit me. Now, she's my great pal. We don't fight anymore because Ms. Sandra said, "Good kids will always share love and joy, and we are good kids, daddy, and Ms. Sandra is the best teacher. I love her so much," says Billy.

The next day, it's almost five in the evening; Sandra finishes her work and calls Merlin, who's playing so far on the seesaw with Billy. She can't hear her mother calling, so Sandra walks fast to take her home as it is getting colder in Houston. "Merlin, come on, we gotta get home. Don't be dawdling; hurry up!" "Hey, buddy, where's your dad? They're gonna close the school in another thirty minutes. Do you have his phone number?" He doesn't know when his father will show up. "Yes, Ms. Sandra." She dials his number and gives it to him. "Hey, dad. It's me, Billy. Where are you? I'm waiting for you. Ms. Sandra and Merlin are leaving, and they are going to close the school soon. It's freezing cold out here. Please come soon, daddy," says Billy. "Oh, my little pumpkin! I'm so sorry, buddy. I'm stuck here in a meeting just a few miles away from your school. I rang your school's phone number many times, but no one answered. What was your Ms. stupid Sandra doing? Was she taking a nap at work? Why didn't she answer the call?" yells George. "Hold on, hold on, dad. The phone is on speaker. She's standing next to me." "Hey, wait, what? Why didn't you tell me that before? Oh…I apologize, Ms. Sandra. I didn't mean any…" She snatches the phone from Billy's hand and says, "Listen, I'm not paid to attend the phone calls, and that's not my duty either. I'm a responsible woman and a mother; I didn't want to leave your son all alone on campus, so as a courtesy, I gave him my phone to call you. Now you figure out a way to get your son home." "Jesus, how stupid I am. Please forgive me, Ms. Sandra. I'm totally insane. Please do me a favor. Can you take my son home with you? I'll come to your house in two hours and pick him up," begs George. "You don't know anybody on this earth. Who are you? I can't babysit any irresponsible man's child." George is trying to convince her to take his son home. In the meantime, Billy is crying in fear of being alone on campus. "Alright, I'm not doing it for you but for your son. Please don't come to my house to pick him up. I'll bring him back to school tomorrow morning with my daughter." "Oh, thank you so much, Ms. Sandra. I will…" She disconnects the call abruptly.

Billy is so happy to go with Sandra and Merlin to their house. "Your house looks so beautiful, Ms. Sandra. Thanks for taking me with you! Am I gonna sleep over here?" asks Billy. "Yes, you are," says Merlin. Sandra gives each one of them a glass of milkshake and some cookies; they play board games and watch cartoon shows on television for some time. "Children, playtime is over. Let's take your books and do your homework," says Sandra from the kitchen room, and she also asks Billy if he likes anything specific for dinner. "Well, my dad works at a restaurant;

he usually brings food for both of us, and he hardly ever cooks at home. It's so nice of you to ask my preference. You may prepare anything you'd like to, and I'm okay with it." She pats him gently on his back. The three of them join hands together. Merlin says the prayer, "Bless us, O Lord, and these, Thy gifts, which we are about to receive from Thy bounty through Christ, our Lord. Amen." After dinner, she tucks both the kids into bed and tells them a bedtime story. George has never told him any bedtime stories. All they do is eat out and watch movies, so Billy finds everything new and likes it very much.

The next day at school, George tries to meet Sandra to thank her for accommodating his son, but she purposely refuses to see him to avoid any unnecessary conversation. After waiting for a long time, he understands that she has no interest in meeting him, so he writes a short thank you note on a piece of paper and gives it to her daughter. Sandra doesn't even care to open that paper. "Maa, why didn't you come to meet Mr. George? He seems to be a nice person. He waited in the hallway for more than forty-five minutes for you," says Merlin. "I know whom to meet and whom not to. Now, close your eyes and go to sleep," says Sandra and gently kisses her daughter on the forehead. "Good night, honey."

While coming back home from shopping, Merlin dozes off in the car. "Why does dad hate me so much? Am I ugly? Mommy, can you please tell dad that I love him?" Sandra overhears Merlin's somniloquy, feels her throat closing up, and tears welling up in her eyes. Sandra feels that Merlin is not old enough to neither understand nor handle the truth, and there is no way that she can tell her anything at this moment. But when the time is ripe, she'll spill the beans.

"A new life can never be formed out of Sin, Curse, or Disgust. It's life, and it's pure. It's not about how it starts and how it ends but how one feels and experiences throughout the journey of it. And to be virtuous, one's totally in control of oneself."

Sandra never saw her daughter as a result of her painful past but rather as a gift that would let her recreate her future.

At school, during the annual day celebration, most of the parents will come together with their kids. Some parents would pick up or drop their children at school and wave hands together, even at the hospitals; kids would be sitting between their mothers and fathers. So, every time Merlin sees such things, she asks her mother, "Mom, why doesn't dad ever show up? She mostly diverts her to something else or gives false hope, which would temporarily seal her mouth from talking about it for some time. Sandra tries her best to fill the space of a father in Merlin's life, but it's practically not possible because the father is an important and irreplaceable character in all the children's lives.

"Oh wait, dad! Put your chopsticks down. I know you're hungry, and you like Chinese food, but Ms. Sandra told me that we need to be grateful to God for what he has given us. She said that we need to pray before every meal we have. So, let's pray, daddy!" says Billy. "That's interesting, buddy! Your teacher has taught you some good stuff. I'm so proud of you, my boy." "Yes, daddy. She's a great teacher." "I bet she is," says George.

George hasn't fixed his mechanically sabotaged car yet; he has a hard time paying rent for his apartment, school fees, and other stuff, but he doesn't impose anything on his son. He always tries his best to give what his son likes, but still, most of the time, he ends up failing to meet his wishes. Whenever Billy asked about his mother, he would say, "She's in heaven with God and will only come down to earth if you don't throw tantrums." He uses it as his magical weapon to control Billy. Billy loves his mother so much; he always sleeps with her picture and talks to it whenever he misses her. George doesn't tell him about the tragedy of his mother, hoping that he will eventually get to know the truth as he grows up. He's a gourmet; that might have been a reason why he chose to work at the restaurant. It gets him good pay and food. Even though his real estate business doesn't get him any fortune, he doesn't give up but tirelessly runs after the money. George doesn't have any friends in the city. He only has a sister, who he loves so much. She lives in Wisconsin. They often talk to each other over the phone. He spends all his free time with his son Billy; he loves to hang out with his father, too, because he never says no to food, be it junk or anything.

"Dad, please come! Let's go out. It's so boring sitting here and watching TV all the time," says Billy. "Well, that sounds like a great idea, but we don't have the car now. If you don't mind taking the bus and walking a bit, then I'm in. We shall go downtown," says George. They take the bus and metro, having a nice time together. Both of them are so fond of street food. They buy extra-large ice cream cones for each one of them and hear a loud thunderclap as they hold them in their hands. "Daddy, look up in the sky. The clouds are so dark. It's gonna rain, and we don't even have an umbrella," exclaims Billy. Just as he predicted, barely within a few minutes, it starts raining. They stand under the sunshades of one of the shops on the street, but it doesn't help.

"Please, be prepared, Billy. We are gonna get drenched, but don't worry. You'll be alright," says George.

"Don't worry, dad. Ms. Sandra's apartment is just a few blocks away from here. I know where she lives. Please, call her right now," says Billy in a shivering voice.

"Oh, please, buddy. Don't give me tough jobs like this. You know your daddy very well. I'm not good at it," says George.

"Dad, then when are you going to learn all this? Come on, daddy. Call her right now, please." says Billy.

He calls her cell phone immediately, it drops after a long ring, and can't even reach the voicemail. He tries a couple of times but gets no response. "I told you. It's not gonna work." Billy stares at him with frowned brows, snatches the phone, and types a message: "Hey, Ms. Sandra. Please call me...it's urgent, by Billy." "You will receive a call at any time. Be prepared to take it," says Billy. She calls him back right away. George freaks out and gives the phone back to Billy, but Billy can't speak either, as his teeth are chattering very badly. So, the phone goes back into George's hand. "Hey, hi, what's up...just checking in, if you guys are alright? It's raining cats and dogs! And deluge everywhere. Please stay safe." Billy stamps George's feet very hard with extreme rage. "Alright, we are near your house. Billy has gotten drenched and is shivering. If you could allow us into your house, I'd get him dried up, and we'd leave as soon as it stops raining," says George. "Oh, I'm sorry to hear that. I wish I could help you, but we're not in town. Maybe you can get help from someone else. I'm sorry again."

The doorbell rings. Sandra opens the door to see who's there while she's on the phone with him. There they're standing in front of her; George's got Billy on his shoulder. They both have half-molten ice cream in their hands. Billy sits comfortably by locking his legs around his dad's neck, holding his hair with his left hand, and having the ice cream in his right, which drips all over his dad's head and face. George has an innocent and unimpeachable look; two of his buttons are off-hooked, as his shirt isn't big enough to cover his big fat belly. Sandra's shocked to see them.

"I'm sorry to barge in like this, had no other choice" says George.

"No, Mr. George, you guys are always welcome to my house," says Merlin.

Sandra gets mad at Merlin, but they get in all by themselves without her permission. There are apples, plums, grapes, and strawberries on the dining table. Both of them sit comfortably and start eating the fruits. Sandra doesn't say anything because she doesn't want to hurt Billy. "Hey, Sandra! You got something for us to eat. We only had ice cream, and Billy is hungry," says George. "Oh, is it? Why are you using my name, dad? If you are hungry, just ask her directly. Ms. Sandra is very kind. She'll give you food. And I'm not hungry." says Billy. Sandra looks at George and sighs; Merlin gives each of them a towel and says, "First, get yourselves dried up. My mom will make delicious pasta for all of us."

Later, she brings two plates of pasta and two pieces of cream cake for dessert. She keeps looking out the window, but it still rains. They can actually hear the torrential from inside the house. "Mr. George, why don't you and Billy sleepover? Because I don't think it's gonna stop raining," says Merlin. "That sounds like a great idea," says George happily. Sandra gets upset and says, "I already googled it. It's gonna stop anytime soon."

It's 10 o'clock at night, and it still rains. Billy is fast asleep on the couch with his father. Merlin sleeps in her room.

Sandra lies in her bed and turns round and round, getting a nightmare of Ricardo coming after her. She screams loudly and goes to her daughter's room to check if she's safe. George and Billy are scared. They both run and hide under the dining table. "What happened? Is that a serial killer or a psychopath? Please call 911," cries George in a trembling voice. Sandra has Merlin in her hand and holds her tightly in fear. "Where are you, George, Billy?" calls Merlin. "Mom, look over there. They are hiding under the dining table. Mr. George and Billy, please come out. You guys are safe here. There's no psycho or serial killer. You may come out. My mom usually does this at least once a month, and I'm used to it," says Merlin. They both come out. "I was about to jump out of the window with my son," says George. Sandra and Merlin shrieked with laughter.

Chapter 9

The Fire Accident

"A mind with retaliation can never be at peace, whether or not it could take revenge on a perpetrator. But it has already started destroying the one who is holding it. Forgiving them is the greatest freedom that one can give to oneself. It can certainly flourish the life immersed in the grudge of darkness."

Sandra had forgiven everyone who had ruined her life, but the fear of protecting her daughter keeps her vigilant, so her antipathy toward men is still fresh. She's young and beautiful, but no men would dare to go after her because she's never given them a chance and is always rude to all of them. George likes her despite her impertinent manner. He only spent time with one woman, Lilly, his wife, who passed away six years ago. Since then, he hasn't been in a relationship with anybody. Billy was just five months old when he lost his mother. George's sister, Catherine, helped him to take care of his son Billy until he was two years old. She's his only relative, who he can always count on, but she doesn't live nearby. Catherine is a great mom. Her husband, Laurie, is in the military, so she lives with her two sons, Ernie and Garry, in her in-laws' house in Wisconsin. Catherine's insisted his brother repeatedly to find a partner, not just for himself but for the sake of his son too; still, he shows no sign of interest, nor can he find any woman who could replace his wife. Before he met Sandra, he never used to wear nice clothes. All that he'd been doing after his wife's death was working at the restaurant, doing real estate, finding clients, and eating a lot. Now that he meets Sandra, his attitude and approach toward his life have changed. He wears nice clothes, especially when he picks up or drops his son at school. "Dad, are you okay? Is everything all right?" asks Billy. "Yeah, all good. Why? What happened?" replies George. "No, dad, you are getting smarter and smarter nowadays," says Billy. "Come on, Buddy, don't be jealous," replies George. But Sandra doesn't show any interest in him because she is badly hurt and not ready to trust anybody and go through the same pain all over again.

Billy loves his mother very much; he believes that she's in heaven and will come down to earth one day to celebrate his birthday with him. During recess, he says the same thing to one of his classmates. "Billy, you are so dumb. Dead people can't come back. Your mother is dead, and she'll never return, " says Brian. Billy's face turns red; he punches him in the face. They fight with each other in the corridor. Merlin witnesses it. She immediately runs to her mom to let her know what's going on. It's so evident that both of them are badly hurt, so their parents are called.

After meeting the principal, George meets Billy's class teacher, Ms. Sandra. "I don't think I'm the right person to give you advice on this, but I know the fear of breaking the little one's heart will always refrain the parents from telling the truth and exposing them to the real world. But Billy is a smart kid. Just sit down and talk to him. I'm sure he'll be able to understand," says Sandra. George's so glad to hear those kind words from her.

"Billy, come here, kiddo." He sits on the couch next to his father and comfortably nestles himself into his father's arms. "First of all, let me apologize for whatever happened between you and Brian, and you shouldn't have hit him. Well, that's a different story. We shall deal with that later. I want you to understand the reality. Your mom passed away, and she's with God. She can't come to your birthday, and you can never see her at all. It was my fault. If I'd told you this before, you wouldn't have been involved in that flight in the first place. I'm sorry, son. Just forget what happened in school," says George. "I know, dad. Brian was right. Dead people can't come back alive. I just understood everything today in school." Tears stream down his face, and he gets all snotty while sniveling. George wipes Billy's face with a towel and hugs him tightly. After some time, he looks up at his dad's face and asks him, "Dad, can Ms. Sandra be my mom?" He keeps looking up at his dad's face but doesn't receive any response from him. "I like her a lot, and she takes good care of me, dad." He is glad that his son likes her too. He strongly believes that she can be the right companion for him and a great mother for his son, but he doesn't have an answer to Billy's question now.

Sandra is a great teacher; she understands her students well, especially when they don't pay attention or show a lack of interest. She wouldn't shout at them; instead, she'd talk to them and find out the cause. In one such instance, there's a girl called Angela; she's an active and highly enthusiastic girl, but for the past few days, some changes in her activities and behavior have caught Sandra's attention. At lunch, when everyone eats their food, Angela sits in the corner, folds her hands, and rests her head on the chair's writing pad. Sandra goes to her and touches her forehead to check if she runs a temperature. "Are you alright, Angela? Why didn't you have lunch?" "No, Ms. Sandra, I don't feel like eating. I just wanna be alone for some time," says Angela. Sandra can sense that there's something wrong with her, so she takes her to the student's counseling room, where no one's around. She might feel comfortable and open up. There they sit in the room, just the two of them. "I know you are a strong and brave girl. If there's anything that you wanna talk to me about, I'm always there for you." "But I'm too scared to talk about it," says Angela. She gives her confidence and assurance that nobody can hurt her. All the kids love Sandra, including Angela, so she believes her words. "I don't like my music teacher, Paul Fernandez. He often makes me sit on his lap to teach violin. He says that if I wear underwear, I can't learn fast. In the next class, I should take them off. If I tell this to anybody, I'll be locked in a dark room forever, and he'd kill my mom too. I'm too small to fight with him," says Angela dishearteningly. Sandra freezes, and her heart skips a beat.

She holds Angela's hands and says, "Look into my eyes. I'm gonna do something now. You ready?" "Yes, Ms. Sandra." She closes all the windows, covers them with blinders, and locks the doors. Now, the room had become completely dark. Sandra asks her to stand facing the wall, and she throws her mobile phone flashlight behind Angela. "Now, what do you see on the wall?" asks Sandra. "I see a big shadow of myself, Ms. Sandra," says Angela. "That's the reflection of who you are, and you are bigger than who you think you are. The light you have behind is the Lord, the Almighty; he gives you courage, strength, and confidence. When you are in fear or sorrow of darkness, have God right behind you as your faith, just like this flashlight. You will be stronger than your enemies, wiser than your problems, and braver than your fears. And you can face everything with your chin up," says Sandra motivationally. Now the child looks more confident than before. Sandra tells her the plan to catch the perverted music teacher red-handed. Now Angela is ready to face him fearlessly.

"500,000 to 1.2 million children are involved in child prostitution. One million women and girls work as prostitutes. Most prostitutes have been sexually abused as children. Finkelhor and Browne state that child sexual abuse leads to feelings through the victim of betrayal, powerlessness, stigmatization, and the sense that sex is a commodity. These feelings often make children vulnerable to re-victimization, including child prostitution. 2/3 prostitutes were sexually abused from the age of 3-16. 2/3 of prostitutes abused in childhood were molested by natural, step- or foster fathers. 10% were sexually abused by strangers."

Birthday is an important and favorite day for all the children; Billy always counts the days to his birthday and starts reminding his father two months ahead of time to arrange for a grand party.

"Hey, kiddo! What do you like to do on your birthday? Please let me know who you'd like to invite and where'd you like to celebrate," asks George.

"Just keep it low, daddy. I don't feel like celebrating it, and I don't think I can enjoy my birthday without mommy," says Billy, sitting in the chair with his elbow resting on the table and keeping his hands on his cheek melancholy.

"That's not right, son. I understand how you feel right now, but how about Ms. Sandra and Merlin? We can invite them to your birthday. They like you, and you like them, and I'm sure they'll be glad to attend the party," says George excitedly.

"I know they like me, dad, but Ms. Sandra doesn't like you. I'm sure she won't come to the party." Said Billy

Before Lilly passed away, George made a commitment to her that he would take good care of Billy. He may not be perfect, but he works hard to give the best life to his son and never lets him down at any cost. He doesn't want his son to miss his birthday because he knows how much he likes celebrating it. Somehow, he persuades Billy to have a party and also assures him that Merlin and Sandra will be there without fail. Billy only wants to invite Sandra, Merlin, aunt Catherine, and his cousins to the event. George is on board with Billy's request and loves celebrating his son's birthday with the people he loves the most. However, he finds it challenging to approach Sandra, so he plans to urge Billy to invite her. He has a strong feeling that she won't reject the kid.

He phones his sister Catherine and tells her how excited Billy is to see his aunt and his cousins and also invites her to the birthday party. "I want to introduce you to someone very close to my heart. I think she is the one you've been asking me to find for myself and Billy. Billy also loves her a lot. He was the one who gave me the idea of having the party with just a few of us. He didn't even invite any of his friends," says George. "Wow, that's great news after such a long time. I'm glad that you found one. I can't wait to meet her. I'm gonna book the tickets to Houston right away," says Catherine gleefully. She is so happy now, thinking that her brother is going to get engaged soon, not aware of the fact that it's only him who's interested but not her.

George goes shopping with his son to buy some nice clothes for the party. It has been years since he spent time or money to purchase good attires, but of late or after meeting Sandra, everything changed.

Fortuitously, he gets a glimpse of Sandra and Merlin on the opposite side in the women's section of the shopping mall. George becomes overstrung. He holds his son in one hand and carries the shopping bag in the other. He stands behind the grand beam and peeps out slightly to make sure that they are really Sandra and Merlin. He is right; he indeed saw them. Being afraid of confronting Sandra, he wants to leave the place before she can see him. He strides fast to go somewhere else; he's got the bag in one hand, but the other hand is hanging free. Billy is missing.

"Where is Billy?" He's searching for him everywhere. To his surprise, he shouts back, "Daddy, I'm here. See who I found. Come here, daddy." He's with Merlin and Sandra.

"Oh my god, Billy. You exactly did what I didn't want to happen," says George under his breath.

He walks casually to them and says, "Oh, Billy. You're here. Hey, Sandra! Hey, sweetie pie!" He high-fives Merlin jubilantly.

"I'm celebrating my birthday this Sunday, so my dad and I are shopping now. Ms. Sandra and Merlin, I'm officially inviting you to the party. Your presence is very much appreciated," says Billy.

Merlin is excited to know about his birthday, "Cool, we'll be there before everyone arrives, and I'll get you a nice gift, Billy." Merlin likes George a lot, and he likes her too. She stops asking about her father ever since she met George, which Sandra notices too. Sandra doesn't like to attend any parties; hence, she says, "No, sweetheart. We can't go. Mom has important work to do this Sunday." Billy's face becomes as long as a fiddle. "I won't cut the cake if you guys don't show up," says Billy downheartedly. George tries to convince her, "There won't be much crowd; we're just inviting a few people who are close to our hearts." But Sandra doesn't seem to pay attention to him; Billy looks dejected, folding his hands and facing his head down. Sandra is kind-hearted; she doesn't hurt anybody and is always benignant with kids. She stands on her knees, holding Billy's arms, and looks into his eyes. "Don't worry, Billy. Merlin and I will be there when you cut the cake. I promise." He hugs her promptly, and so does Merlin from behind. As a matter of fact, George is happier than both the kids.

All of them head together to the parking lot, but the ice cream parlor at the corner grabs the heed of the children. The kids shout for ice cream. Sandra drags Merlin trying to pass the shop, but she holds Billy's hand, and he holds George's. All three of them drag Sandra into the parlor; she sits opposite George while the kids sit right next to their parents. Merlin takes the menu and says, "Today, I wanna have my mom's favorite flavor, i.e., strawberry, so two strawberries, please." "Oh, is it, strawberry! It's my favorite, too," says George. Billy interrupts, "Come on, dad. Don't be a liar. You don't have any favorites. You eat whatever's there on your plate." "Thanks for telling them the truth, my son; that was very helpful. Alright, let me tell you all something. I'm taking an oath here. From today onwards, strawberry is going to be my favorite fruit. I'll only eat strawberry ice cream and drink strawberry juice." George has gotten the ice cream all over his hands and beard. The kids eat much better than him. Sandra looks at him and pushes the tissue paper to his side. He wipes his hands and throws them into the bin. He says, "Thank you." She gives him another one and says, "Please, wipe your mouth clean. I bet your dogs like ice cream too and smiled at him." George is on cloud nine because this is the first time she has ever smiled at him.

On the way back home in the car, Billy asks, "Dad, what do you think about Ms. Sandra?"

"What do you think? What?" exclaims George.

"If you marry Ms. Sandra, she'll be my mom, and I can stay with her, right?" asks Billy.

"Oh my god, where do you learn all this? We can't decide anything on our own before getting to know what's there in the other person's mind. Don't dream about anything, son." But he likes what Billy said.

Billy and George are waiting at the George Bush International Airport to meet Catherine and her kids; they haven't seen each other for a year. Billy is excited to see his aunt and cousins. He spots them and runs to her aunt; she hugs and kisses him. She then goes straight to her brother and asks, "Where's she? Why didn't you bring her?" "Hold on, hold on! She's not here now, but don't worry; you're gonna meet her on Billy's birthday."

After thorough research about Angela's family background, Sandra finds that her mother is on the run after killing her husband, who is an alcoholic and a drug dealer. Angela's been taken care of by her aunt since her parents abandoned her. Angela's aunt, Patricia, is an alcoholic too. She has an affair with the same music teacher, so she doesn't trust any allegations about him. That's the reason the child feels helpless and broken.

It's Monday at 4 p.m. As per the plan, Angela goes to the music class believing that God stands right behind her and gives her all the strength to face the demon. She is ready with the automatic secret recording device and a pen camera that Sandra gave her. As she enters the room, Paul is sitting at the piano, waiting for her, pulling his specs to the tip of his nose and having a glance at her lustfully. Angela cleverly fixes the pen on the side pouch of the bag facing the camera outside and places it on the table, focusing perfectly on the piano. He grabs her by the hand and guides her to the chair next to him. As she sits on the chair playing the piano, his hand slides down the side of her neck. While she plays the percussion instrument, his fingers slowly unzip her dress in the back. She musters all of her courage while shivering with terror. She swats his hand away and pushes the chair on him. Sandra is waiting outside the house with the pen camera connected virtually to the laptop and watching it with the cops in the minivan. "It's time to go," says Sandra. They arrive at the scene spontaneously; Angela is so happy to see her teacher and runs fast to her. The cops arrest Paul, and Sandra wants to release the video on social media by covering Angela's identity. Her intention is to create awareness among all people to protect their children from predators like Paul. She refers Angela to the state as her aunt is an alcoholic, and the government can take care of the child.

Merlin is impatiently looking at the clock and waiting for her mom to get home. "Mom, today's Billy's birthday! You forgot. It's getting late. We gotta go now. I promised I'd get him a nice gift, but we didn't even buy anything for him yet," cries Merlin. "Don't worry, sweetheart. We shall get a beautiful present for him." They arrive sharply at 5 pm to attend the party where George's and Catherine's family is already waiting at the gate to invite them. The house is beautifully decorated with balloons, lights, and glittering silver stars, and also written "Welcome Ms. Sandra and Merlin" Sandra is impressed to see the board, but it's just them in the house. No other people are invited. She finds it weird to see the house empty during the party. "Billy, why didn't you call any of your friends?" "No, Ms. Sandra. As my dad already told you in the shopping mall, we only invited a few people we love the most." Garry is almost three years old, and he reminds Sandra of Simon back in Rockville. He looks more like him. She takes him in her hand and hugs him; she behaves as if she has known him for years. Catherine is happy to see the love she has for her son. All the lights are off in the room, except the six candles that are lit on the cake, and everybody sings the birthday song, "Happy birthday to you..." Billy stands in front of the cake before he blows off the candles. Sandra says, "Make a wish, honey."

"I love Ms. Sandra and my friend Merlin; I want to be with them forever," says Billy and blows them off. Sandra's dumbstruck and joins in, clapping hands with everyone else in the room. George has bought Iron man cake as it's his son's favorite Marvel character. Billy was very excited when he first saw it. His dad sets the disposable plates on the table and cuts the cakes into pieces for the guests. Billy becomes impatient to taste it. "Hold on, Billy, patience is a virtue." Then he gets his first piece. George distributes the cake slices to the other kids and his sister. Catherine hands him a piece of cake and says, "Go, give it to her." "Wait, I forgot to tell you something. I'm the one who loves her, but she doesn't. She hates me as much as she hates the roaches." says George. She is chagrined, with a long stare. "You never change," utters Catherine and pulls him aside. "Are you kidding me? You got me imagining your wedding. Now, you're telling me she has no feelings for you? Okay, look. She's a good one; you can't leave this woman. See how happy Billy is," says Catherine.

"It's not a plant to pour some water, show some sunlight, and expect it to grow big. It's love, sis. It's love. What can I do if she doesn't give a damn about me? She doesn't even like to see my face. Alright, she smiled at me once in the ice cream parlor, and it was the only time she'd ever been nice to me. It will happen, Cathy. She'll fall for me, but you gotta trust your brother and give it a time."

"Oh, come on, George! You can't hope for things to happen, but you need to make them happen. You're a good man. Just show her that." She doesn't believe her brother, so she decides to help him out.

With great disappointment, Catherine is waiting for the right time to talk to Sandra to create a good opinion about her brother. He indeed is a nice gentleman, but her past horrible experience in life doesn't allow her to see his good qualities.

There are pictures of Lilly everywhere on the wall. Sandra is amazed to see them. "She looks so pretty! It's sad she had to leave so young," says Sandra. Catherine is actually waiting for the right moment to talk about it. Now, she is glad that Sandra has initiated a conversation about George's past life. They are sitting in a chair on the balcony, having coffee and some snacks.

* * *

Catherine speaks…

Lilly was a clever and beautiful girl; she had been in love with George for over ten years. They didn't know their fairy tale romance would end as soon as they got married. Lilly's mother died of cancer when she was

fifty-nine years old. Her father was devastated and couldn't bear the loss of his wife. A few months later, he died too. After her parent's demise, she went into depression. Thus, we took her with us, and we all lived together like a family even before she got married to my brother. Finally, they both tied the knot. After a few weeks of their married life, Lilly experienced some health complications. She had chest pain when she took a deep breath, coughed, and even laughed. She also found blood in her mucus and decided it was cancer before getting it diagnosed by a medical practitioner. But still, her fear did not allow her to go for a biopsy as what if it was really cancer? Never told us anything in the beginning; whenever we asked, she'd say, just feeling under the weather, but inside she was suffering a lot. It got worse at one point, so she had to go to a nearby hospital to take a PET/CT scan to find out if her fear was really true. After a few visits and checkups, the doctor diagnosed her with lung and bronchus cancer. As he explained the condition, she couldn't hear a word the doctor was saying. Both of her ears were blocked in terror. All she knew was that she had cancer and was in critical condition. She went home with the report and chose not to say anything to her husband because she wanted to spend her remaining life happily with him. It doesn't matter how hard one can try to hide the smoke; it will always find a way out, and so does the truth. Her health started deteriorating. She looked very weak and dull, exactly how she used to look when she lost her parents.

At last, George read her medical report. He felt that the whole world instantly came to a screeching halt, and a ton of bricks had fallen on his head. Lilly wanted to carry George's baby, but unfortunately, the doctor said it would pose a risk to both mom's and infant's lives. She always wanted to have babies with George, at least two for each one of them. But fate had written a different story for them. George knew her deepest desire, so he decided to adopt a child. Lilly was very excited when he told her about his idea. He wanted to adopt either a toddler or a preschooler, but she chose an infant. "I'm not lucky enough to carry my baby in my body. At least, I'll carry him in my hands," said Lilly. The process of adopting an infant was too long and complicated, especially if the parents were diagnosed with cancer, but with the help of an agency, they were able to find one.

"What happened, honey? You look upset. Are you alright?" asked George.

"Honey, can we think it over?" said Lilly.

"Think it over, what?"

"The whole thing!"

"What happened? I don't understand."

"Look, honey, I'm already dying in fear of leaving you, and I can't add another one to it. He deserves a healthy mother, not someone like me. He needs to have both mom and dad. He deserves to have a mom's love, not just for a few months but for decades. So, please call it off. I can't do this to him."

"What are you talking about? We took a lot of effort to get this far, and we almost got him. He's already our child, not technically, but yes, he will be."

"No, George. Please listen to me. I don't think I can make it." She coughed so hard and threw up blood all over him. George panicked and gave medication. He tucked her into bed. "Okay, honey. Don't think about anything. We'll talk tomorrow." He kissed her and said good night.

The next day, she felt better with the medication and good rest. George is an excellent negotiator; he persuaded her to continue with the adoption process. He later called the agency for further documentation procedures. With the help of an excellent lawyer and the agency, they got a cute little baby boy in their hands. She forgot her pain when she got him in her hand and also couldn't accept the reality that she wouldn't be with him for a long time. George took care of Lilly a lot like a child. He tried everything to save her. He sold his hotel, cars, and house for Lilly's treatment, but it didn't pay any good. She couldn't even celebrate her son's first year birthday.

* * *

Catherine cries. Her sob muffles as she covers her face with a handkerchief. "My brother was left alone with a five-month-old baby. He promised Lilly that he would take care of the child well. He has done a great job. My brother is a great father and a great man." Sandra holds her hand and tries to comfort her.

The phone rings.

"Ms. Sandra?" says an unknown voice.

"Yes, speaking," says Sandra.

"Mam, this is Kenneth calling from the Houston Police Department. The criminal who we arrested today is on the run. I advise you to take care of yourself and your family. If there's an emergency, please reach out immediately. If you get any information about the culprit, please report it to us right away at this same number," says the officer.

Sandra's an independent and courageous woman who has fought many battles and faced many predators in her life. To her, this perverted music teacher is nothing more than a rabid rat. Sandra's concerned about her daughter's safety more than confronting the pedophile. Having a six-year-old around and the uncertainty of what's going to happen next upsets her a lot. She feels weak as a mother.

"Who was on the call? You look upset. Is everything alright?" asks Catherine. "No, I'm good. I can handle it. Nothing to worry about," says Sandra and calls, "Merlin, come here, honey. It's getting late. We gotta go home. Momma has to go to work tomorrow. Please hurry up." She could have taken advantage of this situation and stayed back in George's house to protect her daughter and herself, but she'd never do that. Sandra may not be as religious as Sarah, but she copies certain traits of her mother. She never shares her problems with anyone, nor does she expect a shoulder to lean on or kind words from others to soothe her pain.

George comes down to the living room with Merin while Billy plays video games in the playroom. "Why? What happened? I thought you guys would sleep over." "No, I've some important work. I need to leave." Catherine insists Sandra stay for the night, but she doesn't seem convinced. Merlin holds George's leg tightly in both her hands. Sandra looks at her in surprise. Merlin is an obedient and well-behaved kid who always respects her mother's word and has never been adamant. In contrast, she's resisting her mom today. "Do you think you can be without me?" "Just one night, mommy," requests Merlin. Sandra thinks it's a good idea to leave Merlin in George's house. She looks at Merlin and says, "Alright, just for tonight, and it's the first and last time for you. Mommy will come tomorrow and pick you up." She is bouncing up and down in happiness. George is certainly happy to have Merlin with him, but a bit of disappointment is visible in his eyes as Sandra leaves. They sent her off with smiles and waving hands.

Billy comes to the living room to talk to Sandra but he can't find her. "Dad! Where's Ms. Sandra?" asks Billy. "See, this is what happens when you play a video game. You wouldn't know what's happening around you. She left already," says George. "Sorry, dad. I never knew she'd leave," says Billy disappointingly. "Yeah, I, too, never knew that she'd leave. Alright, that's fine. She had to take care of some important stuff back home."

Billy hears the ringtone of Sandra's cell phone. "Dad! See, Ms. Sandra left her phone here. All right, come, let's go and give her the phone," says Billy. "No, let's not disturb her. Please keep it safe. She's gonna come tomorrow to pick up Merlin. We'll give it to her," says George.

"A wise man will use his opportunity wisely. I hope you can read between the lines," says Catherine.

George's face becomes bright with a wide grin. "Hurry up, children. Let's go to Ms. Sandra's house to give her the cell phone," says George.

"Don't be stupid, George. It's no wonder why you haven't been in a relationship for these many years. Leave the children with me and just go by yourself," says Catherine.

"It's easy to say to get the honey from the hive up in the mountain, but who's going to bear the pain of its crude stings?" says George. "It's worth bearing the pain for its golden sweetness, brother," replies Catherine.

"I don't know when my sister became a matchmaker."

"For the records, it's been years since…but this time, I'm determined to get it done. And yes, I'm hooking you up with her. I hope you got that in mind. Now, stop arguing with me and just get going."

George blindly follows his sister's advice without analyzing it but is still nervous and restless about how to invade her privacy. He is in his sweatshirt and a Capri with a car key spinning on his index finger and says bye to them.

"What? Are you working for Uber Eats, delivering lunch or something?" sighs Catherine. She gives him a brown coat with a turtle-neck t-shirt and black jeans and says, "Good luck, brother!"

Merlin runs toward him, gives him a beautiful red rose, and says, "All the best, Mr. George." He blows her a kiss. "Thank you, honey."

Catherine cries as he leaves the house, "We aren't expecting you tonight. We have our own plans, so just stay back. I'm gonna lock the door right after you leave, and it will only open tomorrow morning." George is shocked, almost tumbles across the stairs, and cries back, "That's brutal, but love you, sissy."

He leans back in his car seat and holds the steering, with lots of love beaming in his eyes. He turns on the music, "I wanna grow old with you." He sings along and drives to her house. With great expectations, he reaches her apartment, standing impatiently in front of the lift and pressing the button many times to get to the fourth floor where she lives. The lift arrives; he hops into it enthusiastically, takes out the rose from the coat, and holds it firmly in both hands. He presses the doorbell with fear and hesitation, turns, and leans on his back against the door with the rose in his hand. Sandra has been anxious since she got the phone call from the officer. She is on high alert, got a hammer in her hand, and prepares to bash whoever is hiding behind the door. She carefully looks through the peephole to check who's standing outside. As George rests his back on the door, he covers the hole with his head, which makes it difficult for her to see through it. She grows more suspicious. Well-prepared has a weapon in her right hand, and promptly unlatches the knobs. He suspends his entire body weight on the door. As soon as it opens, George loses his balance, falls on his back, and drops the rose onto the floor. They both scream at each other. She's got the hammer up in the air over her head to bang him on. George is terrified to see her with the weapon.

"Stop, stop. Please, don't kill me," cries George.

"What are you doing here?" asks Sandra.

"You left your phone at my house, so I just dropped by to give it to you," says George nervously.

"You could've given it to me in school tomorrow," says Sandra.

George is still on the floor and extends his hand to help him out. "Seriously, just get up, George." He gets up by himself.

She stands in front of him, blocking his way to get any further into the house, and tells him to leave immediately. George is so disappointed; he tries to build up a conversation, but she doesn't give any room for that.

"Can I at least get a glass of water, please?"

"Okay," says Sandra.

"I have never been treated this way in anyone's house," George grumbles.

As she leaves to fetch water for him, she accidentally stamps the rose that he dropped on the floor, but she didn't notice it.

George feels bad and takes the flower and keeps it in his pocket."

So... are you alone tonight?" asks George.

"What?" asks Sandra Shockingly.

"No, no... don't get me wrong. Just asked, if you are by yourself or you have any security guard," responds George.

"Oh is it? yeah, I just spoke with the Royal family in Buckingham palace. They are gonna send the queen's security guards."

George looks perplexed and says, "Oh that's great. Well, maybe I can be your security guy until they arrive."

"Oh George, please don't be a pain in the neck. I'm not in the mood to have a conversation with you. Please have the water and leave now. I won't go to school tomorrow, so please drop Merlin off at school. I'll pick her up in the evening. Thank you" says Sandra, and doesn't even offer him a seat.

George looks into her eyes for a moment. Without saying anything, he leaves the place. Her actions have renewed another poignancy of sadness for him. He gets into the lift to go down. No sooner does the elevator close than he hears a loud scream from her room. Instantaneously, he senses it is Sandra, and there's something wrong. He bangs the elevator door open and presses all the buttons, but nothing works. It reaches the ground floor and stands still.

"I'm warning you. Just get out of my house; otherwise, I'll smash your head with this forge," says Sandra. Her heart is cold. Her voice is relentless, unmoved, and stern with every word she speaks, for she knows she has to face this situation undoubtedly.

"I lost my reputation because of you, and you ruined everything. I won't spare your life," blusters Paul.

Much to her surprise, he swats the hammer away and thrusts her so violently against the altar that the big candles from it fall onto the curtains; it immediately catches fire and spreads all across the house. More than 50% of the interior is furnished with wood, so the house is in flames. A burning portiere has fallen over Paul. It covers his body and traps him within it. He screams, blindly runs into the blaze from the furniture, and starts burning right in front of her eyes. She's surrounded by giant flames and hollering for help.

George can hear her screaming and feel the heat as if he stands near the volcano. He doesn't want to waste even a second. He scales the flight of steps as fast as he can and breaks open the door. Without giving a second thought, he closes his face with his two arms and runs into the room. His instincts are right. There she stands in the corner of the room with her gown on fire. He rushes toward her and quickly holds the dress to his left, and swats the flames in his bare right hand. Despite his great effort, he couldn't quench the fire. With no other option, he tears her gown and pulls it off. He takes her in his arms and kicks open the door to the balcony. Sandra can't respond to anything as she is in great shock. Luckily, one of the neighbors has already called the fire department. The thick, billowing smoke captivates the entire block. Parents are carrying their infants, men, women, children, and elders; all are fleeing in terror. The fire truck arrives on time, and the rescuers evacuate everyone safely from the buildings; the panicked populace has congregated across the street. The commotion around the area has never seemed to settle, as no one has witnessed such an incident in their lifetime.

The fire engine started splashing water with the powerful nozzle into the building. It's very cold outside. Sandra finds it embarrassing to face him at the same time; she is grateful for his return. They hear fire marshals coming in. George's coat caught fire, too, so he has to throw it off. Her hands and legs are trembling in the harsh weather. He's left with his turtle-neck t-shirt and pants, which are also half burned but good enough to protect one's honor. He hurriedly removes his clothes and hands them over to Sandra; she reluctantly wears them, and now, he's left with his boxer in the freezing cold. She's shocked to see him; he's badly injured but pretends to be normal.

The huge crowd outside the apartment still watches the smoke engulf the clouds while the fire brigades fight fervently, trying to put out the untamable giant. After hours of tedious work, the men have got things under control to allow the cops to do their work.

Police enter and seal the house as there is a dead body inside. George is terribly injured on his right hand, right leg, and lower back. Fortunately, Sandra is safe without any injuries but is coping with the trauma. Ambulances rush to the scene and take George to the hospital; he is admitted to the emergency unit. Catherine comes with all the kids to visit her brother. His wounds are being treated. He gets discharged from the hospital. Since Sandra and her daughter have nowhere to go, they will have to crash at George's house.

"Thanks, Cathy! If you hadn't told me, I wouldn't have gone there. I can't imagine what'd have happened to Sandra," Says George.

"She's a good soul, and you guys are meant to be together. That's why I'd been pushing you to go to her from the get-go," says Catherine.

As per the doctor, it would take a few weeks for him to recover completely. So, George asks her sister to stay with him for another couple of weeks to help him out. "I wish I could help you, George, but the kids have got to go to school. They'd already taken many days of leave. And it's been more than ten days since I came. I need to leave. I'm sorry, George," says Catherine convincingly. Actually, she purposely leaves for Wisconsin because she doesn't want to be a hindrance between George and Sandra. Now Sandra has to take care of him and the children, and that's Catherine's intention too.

Chapter 10

A Sensible Match

Sometimes, pain can also give pleasure, which becomes true in George's case. He's very happy with his injuries as it brings him closer to Sandra, and he's enjoying each and every moment with her as well as Merlin.

Sandra brings a bowl of hot water and a cotton cloth to wipe his body. Merlin rushes there and says, "Mommy, give it to me, please. I want to help Mr. George. Please, mommy, please." "Calm down, sweetheart. I appreciate your interest, but you're not old enough to do this. You may hurt him and delay the recovery period. Maybe this time you can see how I am doing. After a few days, you can help him as you wish." She runs away to play with Billy. Sandra gently wipes his body and gives him a little massage. Luckily he only has a mild first-degree burn but severe back strains and sprains. George can't believe what's happening right now. This is the moment that he's been waiting for. He finds it very soothing and feels every pressure she applies to his body.

At dawn, the ecstasy of the sun greets the entire city of Houston. The warm and fussy light shines brightly on Sandra's face through the window. She bounces back on her feet; she can rejuvenate herself from any situation or problem, just like a phoenix.

"Coffee, breakfast, and lunch; everything is ready on the table. Please help yourself. Call me if you need anything. I have some paperwork to finish in school, so I gotta go now," says Sandra. "I feel bad for having you do all these; I'll be alright in the next two days. After that, I'll be able to do everything by myself. Thanks indeed," says George.

"If you hadn't come there the other day, I would have been burned in the fire, and my daughter would've ended as an orphan. You risked your life to save me; if I'm alive now, it's only because of you. It's my turn to help you, so please allow me to do my duty. Yes, once you fully recovered, we'd leave," says Sandra. She kisses both Merlin and Billy and leaves for school.

At 1 o'clock, she goes to a restaurant to have lunch since she hasn't brought it from home. It's a busy day. The food court is fully crowded, and there are no seats available. So she orders an icy coke and a Big Mac, as she's got no time to wait. There's another shop next to where she is. People are standing in a queue to get some takeaway; Sandra is keen on a girl and a man who's standing behind her. It looks like the man is whispering something sexually abusive to her ears and also trying to touch her voluntarily, which makes her feel uncomfortable.

The girl is literally shaking and crying but not moving from that spot. It's a busy place where hundreds of people are passing by; no one is either witnessing or trying to intrude. They are heading toward their work, busy browsing their cell phones or listening to music. It looks obvious that the man's trying to misbehave with the girl in her late twenties. Sandra immediately jumps into the scene and says, "Hey, there! What's up? It's been a while, isn't it? How are you doing?" The girl looks confused. Sandra stretches out her hand and says, "Come, let's have lunch together. My table is over there." Now, the girl realizes that Sandra's trying to help her. "Thank you so much for stepping in, ma'am. By the way, my name is Kelly. He'd been following me from the subway with a few cat callings. I didn't know how to get rid of him, so I joined this line, though I got nothing to buy." "Why do you have to go through all this? It's daylight and just look around. There are people everywhere. Why were you so reluctant? Why didn't you stand up for yourself?" asks Sandra. "I understand, but I had no courage to confront him. I just wanted to lose him and get away from the situation; that was all I had in my mind. A girl like me has this sort of dogma, as harassment and abuse are inevitable for us. If I fight with him today, I will probably have to fight with another guy tomorrow. I don't think I have the energy to deal with people like him every day, so I choose to untangle myself and try everything it takes to get rid of that maggot." Sandra videotapes the entire incident with a clear image of the accused and asks Kelly if she can upload it to social media with her face blurred. Kelly tells Sandra not to mask her face and is willing to tell people exactly what happened and how vulnerable she felt while facing such an incident alone.

After the lunch break, Sandra's back at her desk, engrossed in thoughts. At her next seat, there's a woman called Julia, Sandra's co-worker,

"Hey, Sandra! Are you alright?"

"Yeah, I'm good," says Sandra.

"No, you're not. You don't look like how you came in this morning. Something is worrying you! Is Merlin okay?" asks Julia.

Sandra explains what happened outside during the lunch break, but Julia doesn't seem surprised. "Oh, is that what makes you get worried? Come on, Sandra! It's a part of our life to face such injustice. Do you know what happened to me today?" Julia continues, "I have gone through a similar situation on the metro."

The same day in the morning, Julia had left her car for routine service, so she had to take the metro to work. It was about 8.30 am, and the compartment was almost full. She had a handbag on her shoulder and some files in her left hand, holding the bar on her right for support. While listening to music in her own world, a strong cigarette smell invaded her privacy. She tried to see who was behind her with squinted eyes. Suddenly, he got his hand around her hip, pretending to be holding the same bar but pressing and rubbing on her.

"It was disgusting. I didn't know what to do. I felt handicapped at that moment. The fear of what was going to happen next and the fear of being followed and attacked made me avoid escalating it. Girls and women like me may or may not have the courage to fight for ourselves, but we definitely have the ability to tolerate them," says Julia.

Sandra reads a lot of articles and talks to more women and girls about their bitter experiences, but she can't forget the story of the girl called Martha.

"A couple of years ago, I was on public transport to the library. It was 7 am, and the bus was barely filled. I took a seat next to the window as usual and read a book; a man in his mid-forties boarded the bus and occupied the seat next to me. It was so uncomfortable. Although there were many empty seats on the bus, he purposely chose to sit there. I can't explain how I felt, and something was constantly telling me that he was going to hurt me. He was going to hurt me. He pulled out a magazine full of pornographic pictures, pushing me with his elbow. He grabbed my hand tightly. His pants were unzipped and made me hold his thing. I was coerced to do it, and it was absolutely disgusting. I got my hand wet and dirty; I walked away with shame and guilt. I still don't know why I felt guilty or ashamed of myself in spite of being innocent. There were no ears to trust and no courage to tell anyone about what happened to me. I'm black and a foster child, so I thought I was targeted, and every black girl must go through this. But one day, I happened to talk to one of my white friends about it, and she shared her story of sexual harassment; then, I realized it's not about color but gender. The younger and underprivileged you are, the more vulnerable you could be. Because of his two minutes of pleasure, I had to go through two years of depression. Luckily, I was referred to a counselor who helped me to slough off the depression that had been weighing on me for ages," said Martha.

> **"It may be inevitable to face injustice or to go through traumatic incidents in our life, but to come out of it is totally in our control. Seek out help, talk to people you trust, and remind yourself that you do not deserve to go through such pain and don't have to handle it alone."**

Sandra's concern about sexual harassment grows more and more. "How to stop all this? Who's going to change all this? Why can't I? I must do something about it," thinks Sandra.

Sandra clearly knows that the articles she has read and the interviews she has had are just a few drops of the ocean. There are thousands and thousands of victims across the country and across the globe whose stories are still unheard. She's determined to have those men punished and humiliated and make them feel ashamed for what they've done. But more than retribution, she wants to find a real solution to this problem.

After a long day, she reaches home. "Mommy!" "Ms. Sandra." Both kids run toward her while George is resting on the couch. "How are you, George?" asks Sandra compassionately. "Yeah, getting better, and how was your day?" asks George. "Yeah, it was good. I got some medicines for you from the pharmacy," says Sandra. She helps him apply the cream to his lower back and places where he's injured. "I'm glad that you are recovering fast; it seems that maybe in another few days, you'll be completely alright. Then Merlin and I would move to a different place because I don't want to be a burden for you anymore," says Sandra. "We would love to have you guys here, and it's our pleasure to be with you and Merlin. It's not a burden at all. Please don't say that. You know how happy Billy is to have you guys around," says George.

After dinner, everyone hits the bed except Sandra. She tries to do some research on sexual harassment, and the statistics leave her speechless.

18% of women in the USA have been raped at some point in their lifetime. (*Source: Department of Justice*)

Sexual violence affects millions of Americans. Every seventy-three seconds, an American is sexually assaulted. On an average, there are 433,648 victims (age twelve or older) of rape and sexual assault each year in the United States. One out of every six American women has been the victim of an attempted or completed rape in her lifetime (14.8% completed, 2.8% attempted). (*Source: RAINN*)

Sexual violence can have long-term effects on victims. The likelihood that a person suffers suicidal or depressive thoughts increases after sexual violence. 94% of women, who have been raped, experience symptoms of post-traumatic stress disorder (PTSD) during the two weeks following the rape. 30% of women report symptoms of PTSD nine months after the rape. 33% of women who are raped contemplate suicide. 13% of women who are raped attempt suicide. Approximately 70% of rape or sexual assault victims experienced severe distress. It is a larger percentage than any other violent crime. Native Americans are at the greatest risk of sexual violence. On average, American Indians aged twelve and older experience 5,900 sexual assaults per year. American Indians are twice as likely to experience rape/sexual assault compared to all races. 41% of sexual assaults against American Indians are committed by a stranger, 34% by an acquaintance, and 25% by an intimate or family member. Both women and men who are sexually assaulted are more likely to use drugs than the general public. (*Source: RAINN*)

She spends her entire night doing research on rape and sexual harassment, and she is totally blown away just by looking at the data and statistics. The next morning at the coffee table, she looks so tired, and her eyes are red.

"I saw the lights were on in your room last night. Why were you up the whole night yesterday? Is everything alright?" asks George.

"Yeah, I had to do some research; the results were quite devastating. I couldn't sleep after that," says Sandra.

George is curious to know what it is, and eventually, he gets the answer to his question. He is glad and feels proud that she stands up for violence against women. Sandra tries to find some like-minded persons to join hands in stopping the crime against women. She created a Facebook group called 'YOU ARE NOT ALONE.' She plans to run an awareness campaign with as many volunteers as possible across the country. The main motto of this movement is to empower women and threaten the offenders. They create awareness through music, pictures, paintings, dramas, and role plays. Her initiative has received a massive response from the people. The number of volunteers is increasing across the country. She has also started getting donations from business people and organizations.

Her approach to women's empowerment has grabbed the attention of social media and News channels. She's busy giving interviews and attending meetings. In the meantime, George has also recovered completely.

George wants to start a new life and make a family with her, but he doesn't know how to approach it. One thing he knows for sure is that she has changed a lot more positively since the fire accident. Most of the women in this world have been directly or indirectly victimized. Of course, they all have the intention to stand up for themselves and raise their voices or do something about it, but due to financial or personal reasons, they are choosing to remain tolerant. Only a few of them have the courage to fight off; Sandra is one of the few. George doesn't want her to get distracted because of his proposal. She is on a mission, and the path she has chosen wouldn't be the one that everybody would dare to choose. So, he's suppressing his emotions.

"Mom! Why are you packing things up? Where are we going?" asks Merlin.

"Honey, stop asking me any questions! Go get your things! We are leaving now," says Sandra.

"But mom, why aren't Mr. George and Billy packing their things? Please tell me what you are trying to do," asks Merlin.

"They were so kind to accommodate us, and we shouldn't be a burden to them anymore. God will bless them for their kindness. Now, get your things packed up without asking any further questions," says Sandra.

George is standing right behind them, listening to every word she utters. He gently goes to her, closes the luggage, and pushes it away. "Why are you doing this to us? Do you think we'll be happy without you? and Billy can't bear the pain of loneliness after you vacate." asks George.

"I know it will be difficult for him, and he'd cry sometimes, but you know what? Pain is not permanent; time is the greatest medicine for all wounds. Let it be inside or outside. Please, don't stop me. We gotta leave," says Sandra.

"I've never stopped anybody from doing anything based on my opinion, and I will not stop you either, but what I'm worried about is what caused you to move now. Did my son or I do anything wrong?" asks George.

"No, no, never. I'm leaving because of my daughter; I've taught her to be independent, but now she doesn't look so. I've been watching her get attached to you guys. The stronger she gets fond of you, the harder it will be when she's supposed to be separated. I know where it would lead, and I know my daughter. She can't handle it. I don't want my daughter to undergo any such pain. It's better to stay away, of course, not indelibly. We'd come here to meet Billy, and you guys are always welcome to visit us at any time," says Sandra. "If that's what makes you feel happy, then go ahead. I'm not saying anything, but please tell me where you are going now. At least wait for Billy to get up, or just hold on a second. I'll wake him up," says George. "Stop, stop, please. Wait, don't wake him up. I can't face him. I need to leave before he gets up. I'll text you my new address in Dallas, where I found a job."

She drags Merlin to the car and leaves for Dallas, Texas. Merlin cries all the way from Houston to Dallas in the vehicle and falls asleep.

Billy wakes up and goes straight to Sandra's room, searching for them everywhere in the house. Their wardrobe, cupboards, and bookshelves are all empty. He even goes to the garage to check if her car's there but finds nothing. Billy is desolated and cries. His father rushes and hugs him.

If you are desperate for something which most people have, but you don't, at one point in time, it comes so close to you. You see it, feel it with all your senses, and think you almost have it. But apparently, it disappears all of a sudden. It's too much for a child to be able to handle.

"Why are you crying? They aren't left forever. Ms. Sandra has gotten a new job in Dallas, so she had to leave early in the morning. They said that they miss you a lot. We shall meet them this weekend," says George convincingly.

"Dad, why are you being such a coward? Why can't you tell that you love her and you intend to marry her?" says Billy sobbingly. George goes to the restroom without uttering a word, stands under the shower. The last time he cried was on his wife's death. He remembers what Lilly said before they could adopt Billy. "The child needs a mother. He deserves her love." "I'm not a good father to you, Billy. I screwed up your life. I snatched your moments, your moments with your mom. If I weren't the one, some other couples would've adopted you and given you a wonderful life. I'm to be blamed for everything. I'm sorry, Lilly. I couldn't keep up my promise."

Sandra stops the car by the restaurant to have breakfast. Merlin wakes up and asks, "Mom, where are we now, and where are we heading to?" "Let's have breakfast first, and then I'll answer all of your questions." Sandra knows that

Merlin is upset now. She can understand her pain because she had gone through the same pain when she missed her father in her childhood. She orders her favorite food for the morning meal to make her feel happy; "Bagels, French toast, waffles, and hot chocolate milk." "We are invited for an interview," says Sandra. "Interview? I thought you already got a job," says Merlin with a piece of waffle in her mouth. Sandra then explains to her that it is not a job interview. "It's an Ellen show; we are invited by Ellen." says Sandra.

Merlin loves gorillas, and she donates all the money that she has saved in her piggy bank to *theellenfund.org* every year to save gorillas, as they are one of the most endangered animals in the world. She adores Ellen DeGeneres very much because she loves gorillas too and takes a lot of effort to protect them. Moreover, she finds her the funniest person ever. In all the excitement of meeting Ellen in person, she forgets that Billy and George are left behind. "Wow, that's awesome! I've always wanted to meet Ellen DeGeneres and thank her for everything she does to take care of my favorite animal from extinction. Thank you so much, mommy! And, I wanna give a nice gift when we meet her."

Back in Houston, George is spending a long time in the bathroom sitting under the shower. Billy is lying down on the couch and crying while the TV is on. Accidentally, he rolls over the remote control and changes the channel to NBC, where Ellen's program is aired. As he recognizes

Sandra's voice, he immediately looks at the TV and shouts, "Dad, come over here. Ms. Sandra and Merlin are on TV." Billy jumps off the couch, and George runs from the shower, fully drenched and dripping water all over the floor. "Please raise the volume. I can't hear anything," says George.

"You have around 3.5 million volunteers across the country, and it has become a great success, apparently. What's the reason behind the creation of the 'You Are Not Alone' movement? What made you take such an initiative?" says Ellen.

"There's always been an intense pain behind the success of every woman and even for men too. I was brutally raped by three men. They took turns and molested me, didn't care to stop even when I was bleeding. They also used their cigarette stubs on me. To me, getting 3.5 million volunteers across the country doesn't count as success, but the moment I come to know that no woman in this world is sexually assaulted, that'd be the greatest success. I know it's a daydream, but at least if my effort brings the number of victims down, I'll be very happy about it. My next plan is to extend this movement to India, Pakistan, Latin American countries, and eventually to Europe and all across the world," says Sandra.

"That's so great to hear. You're so incredible! As you said that you're a rape victim, how long did you take or how did you come out of it?" asks Ellen.

"First of all, I'd like to call myself a rape survivor rather than a victim. I want to tell my fellow survivors that life doesn't end there. The world is beautiful, life is beautiful, and the people around us are so beautiful. I'd been living with the grudge and pain for many years because the torment I had in my heart and soul was more intense than the pain caused by cigarette burns and bleeding when they rapped me. If you wear dark shady glasses, whatever you see or wherever you see would be dark, and the entire world would look dark too. I was wearing that one, but you know what? It's not difficult to get rid of them if we choose love over hate. When I say choose love, we should love ourselves first, and then our approach toward our life will change automatically," says Sandra.

> *"Just take a moment and think about a person who screwed up your life, even someone who was being rude to you, harassed you, insulted you, or embarrassed you in front of a bunch of people. Do you think they would give a damn about you? Certainly not. They would be happy with their lives and probably would be screwing up someone else's life or might have changed into a better person, but they'd never spend a second thinking about you. No one would because they all have so many things going on in their lives. It's just you who are so concerned about it. Look in the mirror and*

ask yourself, "What am I doing now? Why am I still contemplating it?

Do you want to grow out of it or keep winding about it and stay where you are? Time waits for none. You better use it; otherwise, you'd lose it. Remember, it's not just the time you are losing but the most precious part of your life too. The sun rises for everybody, and it's up to you whether to open your arms to feel the warmth or to hide in the darkness."

Merlin hugs her mother and cries. Meanwhile, in Houston, both George and Billy watch the TV with tears in their eyes. They are shocked to know about Sandra's past life, and now George is able to understand why she was so resentful. They continue watching the TV with unwavering attention.

Ellen speaks, "You are courageous, young, and pretty, so I'm curious to know if there's anyone in your life."

"I literally hated all the men before I met this man. Everyone seemed to me as a predator, and so did he. But that one incident changed my perception of men. It gave me hope that there are some men in this world who respect women. Women do not need protection from men, but they need respect. Men should treat women, as how they want to be treated and respect them as fellow human beings. If that happens, then there'll be no need for protection from other men. Three months ago, I was cornered by a man in my house who tried to assault me, and my entire house was on fire. He came there and risked his life to save me from it. If I'm sitting here and talking with you, it's all because of him. His name is George. He gave me hope that there are good people around us, and that conferred me with the courage and motivation to start this 'You Are Not Alone' movement. We have gathered all the wonderful people across the country and trained them on how to intervene if someone is being harassed and also videotape them secretly. We created a website called *www.youarenotalone.com* where the victims or the bystanders can post the videos, and it's open to the public. We also guarantee that the federal department in that jurisdiction will investigate those videos and take necessary actions against the culprits," says Sandra.

"That's really awesome! As I told you earlier, you're such an incredible woman. There's no doubt about it. But you still didn't answer my question," says Ellen.

Sandra bashfully smiles and says, "He's a nice guy and the guy that I trust, but to be honest with you, I don't have anything to say about him now."

> ***"Not everyone is as lucky as Sandra to find a man like George. There are millions of women who do not find the right partner for themselves and end up wasting their time/ age on the wrong person. First of all, a man who does not proclaim your relationship in***

public does not introduce you to his family, does not share his whereabouts or his personal life, and does not bother to listen to your side of the story would not be the right choice for you. It's always good to talk about your goals and interests. Imagine if you fall in love with a gallivanter, but you don't like living out of luggage. How would your life be? And you are adventurous, but your partner doesn't even like going out. How can you find happiness together? Your goal may not have to match with your partner's, but you need to make sure he respects it and supports you in achieving your goal. The journey on an unparalleled track will never get you to the destination. Sometimes, he or she may not be the right person for you but could be a better one for someone else, so the problem is not with the other person but with you because you've chosen the wrong person for yourself."

George is so happy to hear that she has a good opinion of him, but he's not sure if that's love or just friendship. On the other hand, Billy is insisting George propose to her. He is not ready to wait till the weekend to meet them. George grabs his cell phone to check if she has sent him the address; yes, she did it already.

"Did you listen to what she said about your dad?"

"Yes, daddy, you're a great man. I'm proud of you."

"Alright, we're going to meet them this weekend. Be ready," says George.

"Why? What are you waiting for, dad? Let's go right now. I'm all set."

"Yeah, that sounds like a good idea. But do we need to inform Sandra that we are visiting them tonight?" asks George confusingly.

"Come on, pops. Let it be a surprise! And if they're not there, that's okay. I'll sleep in the car, and you are on the porch. I'm sure they'll have one," says Billy.

On the way to Dallas, George drives the car, and Billy rides shotgun, listening to music and having fun. They are excited to visit Sandra and Merlin. Suddenly, George stops the music and asks, "Why're you so obsessed with Ms. Sandra?"

Billy pauses and says, "You know, dad, for all these years, I believed that one day, I'd meet my mom and celebrate my birthday and all the festivals with her, but I was so dumb, and I actually realized it the day when I had a fight with Brian. Every time when I see my friends with their mothers, I used to be so covetous, but now I'm not jealous anymore because I've got Ms. Sandra. When she attended my birthday party, I felt like she was the one with whom I wanted to celebrate my birthday."

Even though George is happy about his son's love for Sandra, at the same time, these questions are constantly popping up in his mind. "What if she doesn't accept my proposal? What if she hates me again?" Billy is already feeling miserable as he knows that his mother in the picture is gone forever, yet if Sandra doesn't like George's intention, she'd be parting eternally. Billy will be totally devastated. At least now, she has considered him a good friend, so he doesn't want to screw it up and chooses to go with the flow.

"Dad! Pullover! Pullover!" shouts Billy.

"Why, what happened?" asks George.

"Did you buy the wedding ring, dad?" asks Billy.

"For what, Billy? Why do you need the wedding ring now?" says George.

"Dad, don't be a loser. You can't propose to a girl without a ring, can you? I saw it in many movies where the guy would stand on his knee, extend a cute little box and say, 'Will you marry me?' But, dad, you need to make sure that you get a ring in there and don't show the empty box. And…don't worry, dad. You got me. I'll be your wingman, so don't be nervous," says Billy.

"Billy, please stop being dramatic. We can't afford it now, but I will try to propose to her without it. Do you remember what she said on TV? She's badly hurt already, and I don't want to make it worse. Well, I am not saying no. I will try, but it depends on the situation. Please don't dream of anything. You need to understand things and accept the reality," says George.

After a long conversation and drive, they reach their destination at night. George takes his phone to call Sandra. "What are you doing, dad?" asks Billy. "What do you think I'm doing? I am trying to call her," says George. "No, dad, it has to be a surprise; otherwise, we could have called her before we left Houston. Just go and hit the doorbell, dad," says Billy. He's double-checking the door number to ensure he's pressing the right one.

The bell rings.

"Who's that at this time?" Sandra grumbles. She walks to the door and looks through the peephole.

"Oh my god, what are they doing here now?" says Sandra shockingly and rushes to the dressing room.

Billy presses the bell again, and this time, Merlin pushes a chair to the door, looks through the peephole, and shouts to her mom, "Mr. George and Billy are here."

"Honey, please wait. Don't open the door. Hold on a moment. Mumma will be there. Please wait," cries Sandra. They paid her a surprise visit a few times when she was in Houston, but now she finds it different and can't understand what's going on with her. "Why am I acting so weird? Why can't I just open the door casually?" She is standing in front of the dressing-table mirror and wondering what to do, looking at all the make-up items:

lip gloss, foundation, brown kit, mascara, setting spray, bronzer, and blush. She sighs and pushes everything away. She thinks that the physical attraction will fade away as it only relies on the person's beauty, but the good character would leave a long-lasting impression.

"The eyes of other people shouldn't determine how beautiful you are; instead, it's how you feel about yourself that defines how amazing you are as a person. It's not a good idea to choose your body to win a man's heart to start a relationship. It's nothing but trading like a business. They will use the product until they get bored. Once it is done, or if they find another product that is better than the existing one, they will move on to the new one (in the commercial world, women are referred to or treated as products). If they are attracted to the character of the person, they won't lose that person at any cost. Rather, they would try hard to protect the relationship because beauties are replaceable, but the characters are not. It's unique.

In 2019, a South African model Zozibini Tunzi had crowned Miss Universe. She was one of the most beautiful women who had participated in the competition. What was really amazing about her was that she appeared in her natural afro-textured hair because she wanted to show the world who she was and believed in herself. Beauty is not determined by the shape of your body, the size of your lips, the shape of your nose, or the color of your skin, but the character and attitude, your attitude toward nature, your attitude toward animals, your attitude toward other people regardless of their color, age, gender, religion, caste, and financial status."

Merlin stands outside the dressing room and bangs on the door. "Mommy, are you alright? What are you doing? They are waiting outside. Please go and open the door before they go back to Houston."

Finally, she comes out of the room and looks the same as how she got inside. Merlin is puzzled and thinks that her mother's gone crazy.

"Okay, now please go and open the door," says Sandra.

"Mom, that's what I wanted to do in the first place, but you were the one who stopped me. Alright, I'm going."

The door opens.

"Hello, Ms. Sandra. I missed you a lot. Why did you leave me?" cries Billy. She hugs him and says, "I'm just relocated. You're still my favorite kid." Merlin runs to George; he takes her in his hand and hugs her warmly. She is very happy to meet him again. Both the kids go inside the house while George is still standing outside the door, gazing at her and struggling to take his eyes off her. He trips over the heart of her natural beauty. Now, nothing matters but her gorgeous eyes. She waves her hand at him to grab his attention. He is completely flattered by her pulchritude. "I don't like surprise guests. Anyway, do you wanna come in?" says Sandra with her hands folded.

"Oh yes, I'd love to," says George and gets in. Merlin takes him to the couch where Billy's sitting comfortably.

"Guys, please refresh and change yourselves. Honey, show them the restroom," says Sandra.

"But Ms. Sandra, we didn't bring anything to change," says Billy. Sandra looks at George and says, "So, do you want to go back to Houston tonight?"

"No, no. We were very excited to meet you all, so it completely slipped my mind to bring any extra clothes. Don't worry! We'll do a little shopping tomorrow and cover it up," says George.

"I brought a couple of Billy's clothes from Houston for his remembrance because I knew I'd miss him. Billy, sweetheart, please go get that blue bag from that rack. Your white pajamas are in there," says Sandra. They are all sitting on the couch. Merlin runs fast to the rack before Billy can get up. She takes the bag and hands it to him. He opens the bag and takes his pajamas, and there's another one in the same bag. "Dad, look at this. Your PJs are also here. You don't have to drift off in your jeans. Ms. Sandra, did you miss my dad too?" asks Billy. "No, I actually brought that for Merlin. I knew she'd miss your dad. Okay, guys, please give me twenty minutes. I'll get the dinner ready," replies Sandra, and she gets away with it. They all have dinner happily together at the dining table. After dinner, they watch Netflix with a bowl of popcorn. Merlin sits next to George, and Billy sits next to Sandra.

"Let's go to sleep," signals Billy to Merlin. "Mumma, we are sleepy. You guys carry on." They go to bed, leaving them behind in the living room. "Are you all right?" asks Sandra. "I'm getting better," says George.

It starts drizzling outside, and the window is wide open. Sandra feels cold, so she gets up to close it. In the meantime, George tries to shut it, too, as he wants to be polite. Accidentally, she hits him on his back, where he is injured. He holds his upper back and shouts as the pain is unbearable. Sandra feels terribly sorry. She apologizes to him and takes him back to the couch.

"Oh my god, I'm sorry. It was my fault; I should've been more careful. Do you have the medicine with you now?" says Sandra with concern.

"You know me, right? I didn't bring it. It's okay. I can manage," says George.

As she gets up to shut the window, he grabs her hand and drags her back to the couch. He goes to the window again, which is over his head. He tried to lift his hand up to shut it down but couldn't. He feels a sharp pain in his back. Sandra holds his hand and takes him back to the couch. They haven't closed the window, and it's still open. Both of them are looking at the window and laughing at each other.

"A friend of mine has come from India, and she got me Ayurvedic oil, especially for pain relief, because when I was in Houston, I told her about you and the accident," says Sandra. "That's so nice of her, but I don't think I can help myself because it's in the center of my upper back. I can't reach there conveniently," says George. "Oh, I'm sorry, then I can help you if you don't mind," asks Sandra. How would he deny that? "I don't mind it at all. I'd love that," says George. In a matter of a second, he removes his top and lies down on his stomach on the couch. She pours a little oil on his back and starts rubbing it back and forth. He starts to enjoy it as it feels very warm.

According to Sandra, sex is the most painful and unpleasant act she has ever experienced in her life; the divine feeling one can attain during intimacy has become a curse of torment for many women like her. Knowing her past life and the phases she had gone through have become an indication of a caution signboard to alert George to stay away or even to eradicate the thought of making out. He might be determined not to indulge in lovemaking, yet he couldn't resist her as he felt her close during the massage. He is battling within himself whether or not to approach her but still gracefully splashes eye contact with her. Nevertheless, her beauty has totally conquered him. His biological clock has alarmed and gets his boxer protruding. The magical moment and the rush of chemical reactions in his brain have made him inexorable to make love with her. He's slowly releasing his body and sliding to her, trying to light the bonfire.

Conterminously, she beams at him, which signals the fire has glazed upon her. He fondles her hip and gently pulls her onto the couch. She is increasingly dizzy with this new feeling and lies down on her back, gasping as her heart is pounding. She's so mesmerized that she's not able to take her eyes off him. Undergoing a strange sensation as he caressed her forehead, his whooshing breaths emboldened her shaking knees; she tried to comprehend her body's strange yet unique response. As their eyes get connected and tie them down with invisible threads, George slowly begins to undress, and he sees her distort beyond recognition.

Now the flower has to blossom to let the bee use its nectar but is too shy to do, so George helps her to remove her nightgown only to reveal that she hasn't got any inner garments. She had never expected to find herself cuddling with him, nor did she refuse, whatever it is, but the next few moments are going to redefine their lives and pave the way to an unbreakable bond. She lies down on her back on the full fledge convertible and voluptuous crimson velvet couch. George takes her on him and rubs the silky skin of her naked body with his bare hands, gently hugging her to feel the warmth. In one instance, he becomes ensnared at the first glimpse of her intense, almond-shaped, icy-blue eyes. The aroma of her exquisiteness bedazzles him, but still, her gorgeous fresh red rose petal-like lips distract and grab his attention. His lips can't wait to connect with hers. As he gets closer to her mouth, the heat of Sandra's body rises from foot to head, and her heart skips a beat. He passionately kisses her lips, which parted slightly, allowing his tongue to slip inside. Her whole body tingles. He drapes his arms around her while she runs her fingers through his hair. In the scent of a romance, the blanket of feathery white clouds in the lonely sky has suddenly cleared up and paved the way to the gleaming moon that throws an abundance of light through their unclosed window.

The luminescence of the moon's reflection on Sandra portrays every curve of her body, which becomes even more stimulating for George. The combat that he had and the indescribable feeling ravaged him mercilessly in the beginning. The urge to get it on and to compassionately feel her, but not sure how she would react, was jittering. His genuine love and manliness have won Sandra's trust. As he reaches her beautifully curved bosom and carefully fondles around them, the fluffy, dusk pink areolas long to be tasted and pull his attention magnifically. George bends a bit to take one of them in his mouth; time has stopped completely, and all she feels at this very moment is the kisses of a thousand butterflies. She then instantaneously realizes how precious intimacy is, especially with a person who loves and respects you. Her eyes are half closed as if she is getting high, and her moans have exuberated him to go further and further.

He enters her that gives heavenly pleasure in her treasure chest. She grips the soft pink pillow and begins to ripple on the creaky couch; the sound only adds to the wave on a stormy shore. Her soft moans echoed throughout the room, passionately conveying their citing proclivity.

The aroused feeling has not stopped even after more than an hour. Conscious of what she is doing, she giggles and asks, "Is this an intermission?" He knows exactly what she means and is thrilled to interpret those sweetest words. He guides her hand to his shaft. Not only does he enjoy the euphoria but also knows that she is awestruck and shy. The way she maneuvers it as a gentle toy hardens it more and more. He moans with pleasure. Later, he gestures for her to mount and ride along. Now that the horsewoman is on the roof, they have had a skyrocketing experience. He never thought in his wildest dream, even for a second, that she would comply. It became possible as he behaved like a man. She is now ready to fly along with him. He suppressed all his feelings ever since he lost his wife, Lilly. Now, he can feel that his sex life has been reinvigorated. This physical unification has further kindled the fire in them, resulting in an eruption of volcanic orgasm, submerging them in pleasure as he holds her bouncing bosom that rides in ecstasy. He watches her face flush red, and there is no end to this amazing feeling. The heat of his body, the love and care of his chosen moves, and the attitude of his manliness have yielded to intensify throughout her body and have transcended into her very soul. They have dissolved into one another and forgotten who they are as they smooch exotically. They are all over the moon; this mutually mind-blowing experience can not be described completely in words.

After going through all the suffering in her life, she's finally able to see the light at the end of the tunnel. The intimacy has enhanced their trust in each other while amplifying their love life; it has helped her heal from within. She has now fully emancipated the negative perception of sex and the enmity of men and the entire world. His love and caring touch have rejuvenated every cell of her body. With mutual understanding and having lost her grudge and fear, the sunflower has completely turned toward the sun.

George is a real man, the man who knows how to treat a woman, so he's respectful on the bed too. He wants not only to have sex with her but also to express his deep love for her. Sex is not just about giving or extracting physical pleasure, but it's a harmonious therapy with a phenomenal power to rejuvenate two individuals. With not just interplay but foreplay as well, one soothes the body and mind and enters a whole new dimension. Intercourse should not be like consuming food to satisfy a man's hunger, but rather like a correspondence that should be back and forth to vitalize a healthier relationship. That's why it's called making love, and sex shouldn't be done to show a man's masculinity and prey off a woman like an animal but to genuinely share his adoration through it while allowing the woman to gain satisfaction too.

Everything has happened in the spree of the moment as if it is already destined for them. They are no longer two but one, inseparable in body and in mind. It has been years since she left her guard down, but now she snuggles and sleeps peacefully. George has moistured the droughtiness of her heart, and so did she. The night has become memorable.

The next morning, Sandra is dazzled as a gazelle when the roster in the clock clucks loudly the second time at 7 o'clock in the morning, astounds to see herself nestling on him; she gets up naked, grabs her gown, and runs away to get dressed before the kids can see her. She takes a shower while the children are still sleeping. Then, she wakes him up, "George, get up and get ready. It's already 7.15, and the kids have gotten up. Look at you" He rolls out of the blanket with no clothes on. She gets restless, peeping into the next room to check if they are still sleeping.

With the taste of last night lingering in his mind, he's still floating on cloud nine. He wears his pajamas on as fast as he can. Naturally, she's running late, so she lurks him into the bathroom to get ready. At breakfast, all of them sit around the dining table. While helping her make a sandwich, George tells her not to cook anything, as he plans to take everyone out for lunch, followed by a picnic. Immediately, Billy and Merlin pound on him. They are curious to know which hotel they are going to go to, what they are going to have, and where they are going to spend the rest of their day. He says that he has reserved seats for four at a hotel, and everything else would be a surprise. The kids quietly finish their breakfast while dreaming about their own versions of the fun they are going to have. Sandra wraps things up and starts to work on her project. He quickly cleans the table, empties the trash, and goes about settling the house. "I have an important appointment, so I need to leave now," says Sandra

"But we are going out for lunch and got plans for our day," says George.

"Yes, I remember that. Just text me the hotel address. I'll meet you guys there directly," says Sandra.

At 1 p.m., they all gather at the Hotel Crescent. The host escorts them to their table in the center of the hall, surrounded by other tables already occupied by customers. As soon as they sit, a guy with a guitar arrives at their place with three other violinists standing behind him. A cute little three-year-old dressed up like an angel hands a bunch of flowers to Sandra; she is astonished to see her and the beautiful roses. She gracefully accepts them with a kiss on her cheek. The musicians start playing the romantic song, *Can't live without you*. She enjoys listening to them. However, she is surprised to see everything and can't guess what is going to happen. In no time, the waiter comes with the pre-prepared ice bucket, places it next to the table, and presents the champagne to George, and he gently nods his head with a smile. Sandra and George are nervously looking at each other while the waiter does the process of getting the champagne into the glasses.

The musicians are still playing music at their table. George arises from his chair. People around them are curiously paying attention. "Oh my god! He's going to propose to her," one of them cries, and the rest are still watching him without catching a blink. He comes two steps forward, takes a knee, and gets a lovely little box that has a diamond ring. He gently opens it, shows it to her, and says, "Would you give me the honor to grow old with you until death do us part? Marry me, Sandra." George is on his bended knee. It is all happening too quickly, driving all the way to her place, the unexpected yet memorable physical bond they had last night. Now, the proposal has made her feel breathless. She's now scared because whatever happened from last night until this very moment is too good to be true but happened fast. She's not ready to either say yes or no; now, her only focus in life is to accomplish her mission successfully. "George is a nice man indeed, but what if he is a hindrance to accomplishing my dream? Am I getting deviated from my goals? Does he really love me regardless of my past life, or is that just his sympathy for me?" She's absolutely sure that he's not a player, but there's something stopping her from nodding her head, which she is not sure about. All these questions are swirling in her mind. She doesn't want to make any decisions as she can't think straight. On the other hand, George is still on his knee, waiting for her answer. Everyone is looking at them with great curiosity, and some start shouting, "Say yes! Say yes! Accept it! Come on, Ms. He seems to be a nice gentleman."

While keeping her goals in mind yet unable to forget the union of their bodies, she stands up and embarrassingly says, "I'm so sorry, George." She dissipates. George looks at the ring and the people around him. The entire crowd deflates and gets back to their business. He sportively stands up and joins the kids, who are keenly noticing every bit of it. They are certainly very upset too. "What happened, Mr. George? Why did mom leave?" "Where did she go?" asks Merlin. "Don't worry, children. She's gonna come back. We are still here." Merlin doesn't seem to be understood, and George reassures her, "Mommy needs to use the ladies' room, and that's why she left in a hurry. See, her purse is still here."

"Dad, what's happening? Why did she leave? She doesn't want to marry you, does she? Please tell me the truth," says Billy disheartened.

"Hold on, hold on. I can only answer one question at a time, but that too, not now. One thing I can assure you for sure. She likes your dad. No, she loves your dad very much, very, very much. Well, let's give her some time. She'd come around. Do you think your dad isn't handsome enough to win a woman's heart?" asks George.

"George, you are way cooler than Derik in my class. He's cute, though," claims Merlin. "Did you say Derik?

He's a dumbass sidekick. No one likes him," says Billy. "Billy, watch your words," disciplines George. Kids are arguing with each other. But George is very upset with her response to his proposal. He's absolutely sure that the kind of bond he had with her during the night was real, and every move of her body had accepted his proposal, yet he's not able to understand why she refused to marry him. Inwardly, he knows that he has overstepped it and is willing to go to any extent to get it straightened out. He asks himself, "Could it be her opinion with men that drove her away? Could it be her past life? Does she really trust me?" He's desperate to know the reason why she hasn't accepted his proposal. In spite of all this happening inside himself, he pretends to be totally normal in front of the kids to keep them happy, yet the air of malaise is still taunting him. One thing he knows for sure is that he can't afford to lose her from his life at any cost. Time is ticking away, but Sandra hasn't come back yet. George is worried and is about to go check on her. There's a wide grin on Billy's face, which shows that she's coming back to the table. Kids are asking, "Where'd you been for a long time? We're hungry and waiting for you." "Come on, dad. Let's order something before I get famished," says Billy.

They are all back together at the table, and laughter fills the air once again. The starters, the soups, the salad, the main course, and the dessert come in one by one. Gleefully, the items are munched with small talks and jokes. George tries his best to keep the kids entertained.

Smiles flow across, and giggles grow louder, but he can feel that she is not at ease. The last serving is the fortune cookies, and everyone is super excited. "What did you get, mommy?" asks Merlin. The cookie seems to have done the magic. "What did you get, honey?" asks Sandra without responding to Merlin's question. "Billy, you seem to be radiant. What did you get, sweetie?" asks Sandra. George musters his courage, pushes his luck, and asks, "What did you get?" Her face shies away, but her lips speak confidently. "It wouldn't come to pass if I discussed, would it?" Both Billy and Merlin say it together. "That's not fair! We wouldn't tell ours either." They jump on her.

The tension seems to have eased, and George is relieved of his guilt. The check is paid. He says, "Okay, guys! Let's go." "Go where?" asks Billy and Merlin. "I'm gonna take you guys to a very special place, and it's gonna be a surprise," says George. He constantly looks at Sandra to see if she's got anything to say to him, but she's very quiet and doesn't even look at his face. Eyes speak volumes, when one is afraid, guilty, or in love, and the list goes on and on. Sandra's eyes always speak the truth but are not ready to get confronted, so he can't decode it.

Everyone goes to the car; the kids hop onto the back seat. George drives the car while Sandra takes the passenger seat. "Mr. George, please tell us. Where are we going? I don't like suspense," says Merlin. "Yes, dad! At least tell us the name of the place," says Billy. "Oh, come on, Billy. It's all the same," says Merlin. "Alright, whoever wants to know where we're heading, must recite a poem, and that person will get to know the destination of this journey." "Oh my god, I didn't expect this. I'm so tired, Ms. Sandra. I'm gonna fall asleep. Please wake me up when we reach the spot," says Billy. "Alright, guys, relax. You all will know it in another couple of hours, and no one has to fall asleep. Okay, let me sing a song for you all," says George. "Dad, please don't sing because the last time you sang a song, our dogs Runney and Tunney ran away," says Billy. Sandra bursts out laughing. George feels relaxed to see her having fun because she'd been in a state of confusion ever since he proposed to her at the Crescent, and now everyone is having a nice time in the car. "All right folks, listen up. Let's play a quiz," says George. "I think it's time to snooze," says Billy. "Oh, Billy, come on. This is not the kind of quiz you think. It's a fun quiz. Just give it a try kiddo," says George. "I'm in George. Tell us the rules," says Merlin. "That's my girl."

"Perfect, this is how it works. You guys should name any three people you love the most in this world, but you should only tell me the first and last letters of their names. If I guess the names right, then you should blow me a kiss, deal?" "Cool, this sounds fun. I'm in, too," says Billy. George looks at Sandra and says, "Bravo! let's get started." "All right, Mr. George. The first one is S-a, the second one is G-e, and the third one is B-y. Let's see if you can guess them," says Merlin. "Oh, those are the toughest I ever got. Okay, let me give it a try. Ummm, the first one is Sandra, the second one is George, and the third one is Billy. Am I right?" "Mr. George, you're so brilliant!" exclaims Merlin. "I won, so I want my kiss. Come on, blow me a kiss," she leans to the front seat and kisses him. "Billy, now it's your turn. Go ahead, buddy," says George. "Okay, here we go. The first one is S-a, the second one is G-e, and the third one is M-n," says Billy. "Oh boy, those are really challenging! All right, let me try. The first one is Sandra, the second one is George, and the third one is Merlin. Am I right?" "Yes, you are, and you really are a brilliant dad," praises Billy. "Come on, buddy. Give daddy a kiss! I earned it." George shows him his cheek, and he comes forward and kisses him. "Thanks for including my name Billy. I thought you hated me." Says, Merlin. "I don't like you that much, and I mentioned your name because you gave my name in your turn, so I wanted to be polite." Says Billy. "I, too, don't like you that much. I like George, so I told him your name." Says Merlin "Guys! What's happening here? I thought you guys were best friends. Do you remember what Ms. Sandra told you? Good kids will not fight with each other" Again, the kids start arguing with each other; George interrupts, "All right, guys, please stop it! Billy, did everyone get the chance to participate? I feel like someone is still missing, isn't it?" "Yes, mom hasn't asked you the question," cries Merlin. "Yes, dad. Ms. Sandra, come on, let's play."

Sandra looks puzzled and is simply looking through the window, which George's been noticing for a long time. While focusing on driving, George looks at her and says, "I'm ready when you are." "Sorry, I'm not in the mood to ask anyone a question. I just want to sit back and relax," says Sandra. "Please, Mumma. Don't isolate yourself. We are having fun together. Please join us," pleads Merlin. "Alright, I'll do it," says Sandra. Everyone is shouting, "Hurray!!!" "Hold on, people. I don't know how to play the game," says Sandra. "Not a problem! I can explain the whole thing over again to you," says George.

While George explains to Sandra how to play the quiz, both Billy and Merlin are explaining to her too. She's becoming increasingly perplexed and annoyed as all three of them are talking at the same time. "Please stop it, guys, I understood how to play, and that was very helpful," says Sandra. This time George gives her extra instruction because he knows that she loves her mother, so he says, "All of them should be alive." He's getting nervous as he doesn't know if she's going to include his name on the list. He is driving the vehicle tensely while paying attention to her response. "Okay, let me start. The first one is M-n, the second one is B-y, and the third one is…" She takes pauses and looks at him. He holds the steering of the car and strokes it with his fingers. Both the kids are asking, "Who's the third person?" She continues, "The third person's name of the first letter is G, and the last letter is E." George is glad to hear that. The kids are clapping their hands and shouting, "Hurray!" "Calm down, guys! It's my turn now to give the right answer. Well, the first one is Merlin, the second one is Billy, and the third one is me-George." "Dad, you proved it again! You are brilliant!" "Yeah, I got the right answer, so what is the deal, guys?"

asks George. "Yes, Mr. George, mom must kiss you," says Merlin. They both start shouting, "Kiss him, kiss him, kiss him, kiss him!!" "Hold on, hold on, hold on, guys!" Everyone becomes silent. "He's not right. The last one is not George. It's Gailine, my high school teacher, and she's still alive." "No, mom. That's cheating! You're not in touch with her. You don't even have her number with you, and I know you don't like her either," argues Merlin. "It's okay, sweetheart. Leave it. I'm not lucky enough to have at least the smallest place in your mom's heart," says George. Everyone becomes quiet. George plays some music on the car stereos.

"Dad! Pull over! Pull over! I gotta pee. Pullover, dad. Don't get mad if I wet your car," cried Billy. "Okay, okay, hold on. I'm finding a place for you," shouted George. There is a gas station far ahead of them, which grabs Merlin's attention. "Look, Mr. George, a gas station." "Oh yeah, thank you, honey." As soon as the car stops, Billy opens the door and runs out. "Hang on, don't dirty the road, Billy. Wait, I'm also coming. Get your business done inside the toilet." There's an excellent tourist spot with a spectacular landscape behind the service station; it's an open field with a lot of trees and a pond where people gather for fishing and birdwatching. But today, there are just a few people catching fish and watching birds. Some of them are ornithologists. George thinks this is a perfect spot to have a picnic, better than the one that he wanted to take them to. Everyone likes the place and agrees to spend time there. "Dad, I'm hungry. Please, get me something to eat." "What! We just had lunch a couple of hours ago at the hotel. Did you forget that?" says George. "It's okay. We have some snacks and fruits in the car. I'll go get them," says Sandra. "No, no, you please watch the kids. I'll take care of it." George goes to the vehicle to get the food; he also brings a blanket to have a perfect picnic. Kids are so excited and don't want to leave the place. The velvet green grass, fresh air, and the twitters of the birds make the place more magical. George has been observing every bit of Sandra's behavior, and she seems to be preoccupied. He is trying to have a conversation with her to know what exactly stopped her from accepting his marriage proposal, but he can't get a chance to speak as the kids are always around. He's making an arduous effort to prove to herself that he'll be there for her and her daughter for the rest of his life, but he's not sure if she'll listen to him patiently.

The blanket is spread on the lawn, and they all sit around the basket full of fruits, bread, cheese, and juice. Billy would be impatient, especially when he's hungry. Being not able to wait, he pulls the basket to munch on some. Sandra grabs it from him and says, "Honey, let's pray first, and then we shall have the food. It doesn't matter how hungry we are or how much we got in our hands; we should always thank God, who provides food for us and all the species on this planet."

Sandra sits next to George, followed by Merlin and Billy. Everyone joins their hand for prayer except the grownups, so the circle is not complete. "Dad, what are you looking at? Please hold Ms. Sandra's hand. I'm hungry," cries Billy. "Yes, mama, please go ahead. Otherwise, this boy will eat my hand in starvation," says Merlin. Sandra looks at George; he's already extended his hand. Their eyes are locked as they glance at each other. She slowly offers her hand without taking her eyes off him. He holds it gently. As their fingers connect, it reminds them of the intimacy they had last night.

"Heavenly Father, we thank you for the food you have given us; provide food unto everybody. Amen," says Merlin. "What did you pray, Billy?" asks George. "When I closed my eyes, all I saw was the burgers and the pizza. And I asked God to feed me with no further delay," says Billy. "Oh Billy, alright, what did you pray for, sweetheart?" asks George. "I prayed to have many trips like this with you, Mr. George," says Merlin.

Sandra looks at Merlin's face, and it's so true to be nostalgic; a father plays a significant role, especially in the life of a girl child. He's the first person of the opposite gender that a girl falls in love with. His touch, his hug, and his kiss immensely influence and empower the girl to face any tough situation in her life. Merlin has longed for such love, despite Sandra's great care and affection. With tender characteristics, George fills the void that Merlin has had for a long time. Yet Sandra hasn't validated it for some reason.

"Okay, children, the food is served. Please start eating," says Sandra. George is quite hesitant to initiate a conversation with her; he wants the kids to get away and play somewhere else, but they are just sticking around. After having food, George says, "Honey, see here. I got tennikoit and frisbee. Why don't you take Billy there and play with him?" "Wow! That's cool, dad. Merlin, come on. Let's play," says Billy. He somehow managed to send them away. Now both George and Sandra sit side by side with a foot away, facing toward the kids. She gets up when he tries to initiate the conversation, but he promptly grabs her hand and says, "Can I speak with you for a moment?" She pauses and says, "Sure." "Is everything alright? You look confused," says George. "Is that what you wanted to ask?" "No, certainly not. I just want to say that last night was really unforgettable, and it was very, very special for me," says George happily. "Please don't talk about that if that's what you want to discuss. I'm leaving." "Wait, what happened to you? We had a nice time together, hadn't we? You're talking as if you were forced to have sex with me," says George frustratingly. "No, it's not about you, but me. I'm the one to be blamed. I shouldn't have done that. I feel like we moved so fast, and it was too early to have intimacy. Everything happened so quickly. It's not just about me but also my daughter. I'm accountable for her future. I don't want to mess up her life for my own pleasure," says Sandra. "So, do you mean I'll ruin Merlin's future if I come into your life?" "No, I didn't mean that. If I had no trust in you, I wouldn't have slept with you yesterday. It so happened and actually happened very fast, but now I regret that," says Sandra. "Seriously? Did you say regret? You know what! I've been an idiot, hoping you'll understand my love and accept my son and me, but you won't and will never. At least he was living in dreamland with his mother, hugging a picture of her, looking at the sky, and hoping to see her one day, but as a moron, I told him she is no more and will never see him ever, and you will be his mother, you know what? You proved me wrong. Billy is an unlucky kid. He'd never been with his mother and will never be in the future, and he could never experience the mother and son's relationship. I've no idea how to cut him off from you. Nevertheless, it's better to accept reality and move on than to lead a fake life. Anyway, thanks for everything!" George bursts out.

Sandra listens to him patiently without uttering a single word. Being totally distraught, George goes away. But she still sits at the place and looks stressed out; she knows that he's certainly the best of all the men that she's ever encountered in her life. Yet she couldn't say yes to him. She's highly determined to accomplish her dreams and thinks that George could be a distraction. That's why she didn't accept his proposal. All these are pulling her apart. In a trice, both the kids interrupt her contemplation. "Mommy! I'm thirsty. Get me some water, please, please, please." "Yes, Ms. Sandra, for me too. Please!" George is already standing behind them with an icebox full of cold-water bottles and some juice. She takes the box from him and says, "Thank you," without looking at his face.

She then distributes them to the kids and him, but he doesn't take it. He looks very upset.

"Mom, I'm the best in tennikoit. I won four matches," exclaims Merlin. "You know what, Ms. Sandra? For your records, we played ten matches. Now you know who the best is," says Billy. They quarrel with each other, proving one is better than the other. Billy challenges her that if she plays again, she will not win, but George interrupts and say both of them are the best players. "Okay, let's stop the argument. If you think you're the best, then play one more match with me. If I get defeated, then I'll accept that you're the best," says Billy. "No, I don't want to play singles with you, I'll team up with Mr. George, and you're with my mom," says Merlin. "That sounds like a real game. I accept your challenge." Says Billy. But George sulkily refuses to play. "Billy, I'm in. Come, let's go to the court. If they don't show up, then we won by default," says Sandra. "Mr. George, what happened to you? Please don't do this to me. I don't wanna be a loser. Please don't let me down." Merlin starts crying, which forces George to play the match. "I'll never let you down, honey. How can I? A brave girl will never cry. Look at me. We're gonna be the winners, and let them know what we are capable of," says George. "Hurray! Mom, Billy. Mr. George is playing. Let's start the match," shouts Merlin.

"Mr. George, please, don't underestimate my mom; she is a fantastic player. So, you take on my mom, and I'll take care of Billy, alright?" "Aye, Aye, captain!" says George.

The match starts off; they play happily with a little fight and arguments. Well, that's a part of the game. Sandra and George forget everything that's going on between them but focus on the match; that's what true sportsmanship is. The first half of the match is over; both teams have performed well, and the scores are evenly poised. Billy is thirsty and wants to have some water, so they all agree to have a short break for fifteen minutes. "Ms. Sandra, let me tell you a secret; my dad is weak in his left hand, so if you could throw the ring to his weaker side, he'd probably miss it," whispers Billy. It makes sense to her because most of the catches he dropped were on his left. The game continues, and she targets him on his left; George finds it difficult to catch the ring. On one throw, the ring goes extremely wide to his left on the court, and he literally flies to catch it but ends up falling down and spraining his shoulder again. "Mom, what have you done? Look what happened to Mr. George? It's all your fault, mommy. Please, apologize to him," cries Merin. "Oh, I'm so sorry, George. I didn't do it intentionally. Are you okay?" says Sandra. "I'm alright. I think I sprained my shoulder again." The match has been called off. When she tries to hold his hand, he refuses to take her help.

Sandra feels guilty and wants to help him but is quite hesitant due to the cold war between them. "Mr. George, please wait. Come here to the mat," says Merlin. "I'm alright, honey." "No, you are not. If you don't come, I won't talk to you." George goes to Merlin while Sandra gives the ice pack to her daughter. "Mr. George, you don't have to suffer in pain when I'm around," says Merlin. "What if you're not?" asks George. "No, Mr. George. I'll always be around protecting you." "That's so sweet of you, honey. Thank you so much." Says George. She gets George to lie down on his stomach on the mat and gently presses him with her soft hands on his upper back. "Please let me know if I hurt you." "No, honey, you'd never hurt me. I feel very comfortable," says George. "You have to be very careful when you play. See what happened now! And please don't be mad at my mom. She is a very sweet person. She didn't do it deliberately." He gets up on his foot after getting the cold compression. "I feel much better than before. Thanks a lot, sweetheart!"

"Let's pack everything and go to the car," says George. "Okay, dad, now where are we going next? Please tell us." Says Billy. "Yep, certainly. We're going to Dallas. Drop them home and leave for Houston right away," says George. They are totally disappointed, including Sandra, but she doesn't express it. "Dad! It's not fair. We planned to stay with them for two weeks. Did you forget that?" says Billy frustratingly. "Yes, we did. Now the plan has changed. Please, don't argue with me. We are going home, period," says George. He opens the front door for Sandra, but she snatches the car keys and gets into the driver's seat. She doesn't allow him to drive the car as he is injured. "Are we really going back to Dallas?" asks Sandra before she starts the engine. "Yes, we are. Please go ahead," responds George. Everyone is quiet; there's no joy in the car. It is not how it was when they started their trip.

"Mr. George, are you alright? Do you still have pain in your shoulder?" asks Merlin. "No, honey. I'm okay," says George. "Mr. George, may I ask you something, if you don't mind?" says Merlin. "Of course not, sweetheart; what is it?" says George. "Would you hate me when you go back to Houston?" asks Merlin. "No, why do you think like that? I love you, and I love you more than anything else in this world," says George. "Why do you want to go so early? Why don't you stay with us for some more days?" asks Merlin. "Honey, if you want to ask anything, please ask me when we get home. Don't disturb him. You look so tired, close your eyes, and go to sleep," says Sandra.

Merlin is fast asleep while Billy's looking through the window. George's looking at the road through the windshield, and Sandra is driving the car. "Ms. Sandra, can I ask you a question, if you don't mind?" says Billy. "No honey, not at all, please," says Sandra. "I never called anyone mom ever since I was born, so may I call you mom just like Merlin," asks Billy. She immediately looks at George, and he looks at her angrily. "Billy, what's wrong with you? You only had one mom, and she was dead, you understand? Ms. Sandra was your teacher, and now she's just our friend. That's it! You better shut your mouth and sit quietly," bursts George. "Why are you yelling at him? He's a child. He doesn't know anything. Please, don't be rude to him. If you have any problem, deal it with me," says Sandra. "Oh, is it? Don't blame me. It's you who broke his heart. Alright, in fact, I shouldn't have encouraged all this." In the heat of the argument, she loses control of the vehicle, hitting the accelerator so hard instead of the brake. The car gets uncontrollable. George is trying to hold the steering to keep it steady, but it's way beyond anything that can be done. Children are scared and screaming. "Hit the brake! Hit the brake! You're pressing the accelerator instead. Please, hit the brake," shouts George. As she hits the brake, the car suddenly flips, rolls into the bushes, and stops only after colliding against the sycamore. As soon as the collision takes place, all six airbags are inflated. The fact that they are all wearing seat belts saves them from major injuries. Sandra senses there's something wrong. "Smoke, smoke!! Something is burning! Oh my god, the car catches fire," cries Sandra. Smoke comes out of the engine, and the bonnet of the vehicle is flaming literally; Sandra is screaming again, "Please save the children! The car is going to explode. Hurry up, please!" All the doors are jammed; they couldn't open any of them. Due to consternation, the children are unable to remove even their seat belts. George leans into the back seat, manages to open the buckles, breaks the window, and safely pushes the kids out of the car. The front part of the car is burning in high flames, and the fire starts spreading rapidly. In fear of an explosion, George vociferates loudly, "Merlin and Billy, get away from the car. Go and stand behind the tree. Go fast." Kids are scared, crying in terror, and follow what exactly is said. He tries to open the door of the driver's seat but can't. Sandra's legs are struck. Even if the door is open, it'd be challenging to remove her from the car.

"It is going to explode. Don't worry about me. Our children need you. Just leave me here, save yourself, and go to the children. I can't come out of the car, and we are wasting time," cries Sandra. George doesn't pay any heed to her; he kicks the door continuously and breaks the lock, but still, it only opens a quarter of it. He immediately pulls her legs out and pushes her from inside. As soon as she gets out, she leans in and tries to pull him from outside. "Get away right now! Go to the kids. Otherwise, I will not come out, and I mean it," says George fiercely. She goes to the kids, grabs her phone, and calls 911. As George squeezes himself to come out of the narrow opening of the door, the car explodes and throws him out.

The ambulance arrives at the spot-on time and takes them to the hospital. Everyone has minor injuries except George. Sandra has scratches on her head and hands and a mild sprain on her left knee and ankle as her legs got struck. The kids are okay with a few bruises. She gets informed that George is in critical condition and is admitted to the Intensive Care Unit; they ask the receptionist and find out that he is on the third floor. She holds both kids in her hands and limps to the elevator to get to the third floor. Kids are constantly asking her about George and what happened to him. She can't hear what they are saying; she can't even feel her feet on the floor. All she wants now is to see his face and to know that he's all right. She asks the nurse if she can see him but is not allowed, even for a second. No one is allowed to visit the patients in the ICU without permission, which Sandra clearly knows about. Luckily, she meets the Intensivist while waiting outside the emergency room. "He's passed the danger zone, and his condition is stabilizing now. Nothing to worry about." Sandra breathes a sigh of relief after hearing the words "Nothing to worry about." "Could you please allow us to see him? Just for a few minutes. Please, doctor," asks Sandra. "I'm afraid I can't say yes now, though he's out of danger. The treatment is going on, and he's still in observation. You may see him after three hours."

The three hours felt like three decades to Sandra. She's constantly looking at the clock; even a minute takes ages to move. Both Merlin and Billy are lying down on her lap. Merlin is fast asleep while Billy is looking at the ICU door. "Ms. Sandra, would you get mad at me if I tell you something?" says Billy. "No, honey, never; please go ahead," says Sandra. "I love my mom more than anything in the world. I always wanted to meet her. When I realized she was no more, I thought you could be my mom. So I asked my dad to marry you, and I was the one who insisted him to propose to you. It's all my fault. My dad is innocent. I'm sorry for everything, Ms. Sandra," says Billy. "Ms. Sandra, Ms. Sandra," calls the nurse. "Are you the attendee of Mr. George?" "Yes, I'm." "He has gained consciousness and lamenting the name 'Billy.' Is he his son?" "Yes, he is. Shall we see him?" "Of course, but please don't disturb the patient, and don't take too much time." Merlin awakens. Sandra grabs the children in her hands and nervously goes to the glass door. She slowly opens it to make sure he's not disturbed. He has an oxygen mask, and a drip is connected to his left hand's vein. BP and pulse monitor are also running beside his bed. Sandra feels bad and guilty to see him in this position. "It's all because of me. I should have been the one in this bed bearing all the pain," soliloquizes Sandra in tears. Merlin gets emotional, hugs him on his stomach, and cries, "Mr. George, what happened to you? Please get up. Talk to me." Billy is standing close to his father and weeping soberly. He slowly opens his eyes and sees all three of them standing right around him. Sandra holds his hand, and her eyes turn red with tears. He pulls the oxygen mask down and tells her to let go of his hands. "I love you. I love you from the bottom of my heart. I don't know how to prove my love. That's fine. Let's not victimize our children because of our stupidity. Thanks for everything! I'll call Catherine, and she'll take care of me. Life is meant to live and not be hanging up with our bitter past, so please take care of Merlin and move on in your life," says George.

"I can understand everything, and at the same time, I also want to tell you something right now. I feel genuinely happy when you are around me, and the night I spent with you was very special for me as you blossomed into every cell of my body. You're the real man who knows how to treat a woman, even in bed. I respect you for who you are and what you did to my daughter and me.

You are the kind of man I always wanted Merlin to grow up with. I wasn't lucky enough to spend time with my dad, I don't want to separate Merlin from you. She loves you; she loves you as how I loved my dad. She misses you as how I missed my dad when he was no longer with me. She deserves you, George. You were right in the car; you asked me the three people that I love the most in this world. I said Merlin, Billy, and my third name was you. You guessed it right. I love you and Billy, but when you proposed to me at the restaurant. The other side of me didn't want to accept it because I thought you would be a boulder on my way to reaching my goal. I've always wanted to protect myself and my daughter from the outside world, and it was not easy for me to make the decision right away. I'm so sorry to put you in this situation," says Sandra.

Although his whole body hurts, George holds her hand and asks her to come closer as he's not able to speak loudly, "Do you think I'll be an obstacle to your goal? I'm proud of what you are doing, and I want to be a part of it, and I will do anything to help you achieve it." Says George promisingly.

"Mr. George, just stop talking! What are you waiting for? It was you, the third name," cries Merlin. "Yes, dad, you proved again; you're brilliant. You guessed it right," cries Billy. "Mommy has to kiss you now. The deal is a deal." Both kids say together. George looks into her eyes, and he finds it difficult to come forward, so Sandra leans down and kisses him on his lips. Billy and Merlin shouts "Hurray!" and clap their hands joyfully.

"Not everyone is bad, and not everyone is good. Not everything is right, and not everything is wrong. Likes and dislikes are purely based on the results of the experiences in our lives. It's not fair to say all the mangoes are sour just because we had one or maybe two or even a few. The point is we should know that there are some good mangoes too. Likewise, you might have chosen the wrong boyfriend or girlfriend or even any relationship for that matter; just look at the bright side. Now, you know they are not good for you, so just discard them and move on in your life. Do not stigmatize the entire group and be a product of your bitter experience. First, forgive yourself. Forgive yourself for the fact that you have chosen the wrong person. Forgive yourself for spending all your precious time in a toxic relationship. It's never been too late for anything, but what really is, putting off the right decision. Once you realize it's a rattlesnake, just back off. It could be anybody, be it your friends, colleagues, husband, wife, or even your own family members. If the relationship is toxic, your life will be miserable, so stay away from those people, whoever they

are. Remember, you are not just wasting time, but the most important part of your life too. It takes a certain amount of courage to forgive and move on in our lives, but once you do that, it will be awesome, and you will be able to "Recreate Your Life With Love."